HEARTS OF THE WEST

His Untamed Heart

The Cowboy's Christmas Reunion

By Jennifer Lewis

1

Tara Kent's mind jumped and buzzed like the fly she tried to swat away. This was a beautiful wedding, but she'd never felt more miserable in her life.

Her own wedding, planned down to the most meticulous detail, was postponed indefinitely.

Not postponed Tara, canceled. It's over, finished, no more.

She felt lost and alone. A little out of control. Shivering in her tight fitting suit in the spring breeze.

Then she saw him.

"Oh, no." Her heart dropped right into her uncomfortable high-heeled shoes. And started pounding—hard. "You didn't."

Her friend Melody turned and followed her gaze to where it had landed on a tall, rugged cowboy, daringly dressed for the most elegant wedding of the year in a black tuxedo with jeans and boots. *Jesse West.*

"Don't be silly, darling. He's an old friend."

"Of mine. Not yours!" Melody had only met him for a few days during a working trip to Vegas two years ago. A trip during which Melody boldly seduced their wealthy client, who had, just minutes earlier, become her fourth husband.

"It's my wedding. I can invite whoever I want. He's from one of the oldest and richest families in

Texas. I enjoy having the crème de la crème on my guest list." Melody sipped her champagne and gestured to the gathered crowd of elegant guests swaying to a live band on the lawn of Austin's most magnificent estate.

"How did you even get his number?"

"I can get anything, darling. I have contacts. His brother Bowie is here, too, with his adorable new fiancée, Lucy."

Tara blinked. "I can't believe you'd do this to me. I'm sure he hates me."

"Jesse? Don't be silly, darling. It was just a fun Vegas fling."

That Melody had talked her into. She'd regretted it daily ever since. Especially since she'd come home to a long-awaited proposal from her ex-boyfriend, which she'd tearfully accepted.

Jesse stood a little apart from the others, watching the dancers with the faintest hint of a smile playing around the corners of his mouth. He carried himself easily, arms crossed over his chest, taking in the scene around him as if he were invisible.

Suddenly his dark eyes flicked toward hers and transfixed her with their gaze. A flash of heat shot through her body. She gasped audibly and looked away, willing herself not to look back at him and see if he was still watching her.

The afterimage of him burned in her retinas, his unstyled black-brown hair, his high cheekbones, that half-smiling mouth and damn those eyes.

"I saw that! Goodness, he made you breathless." Melody chuckled while Tara struggled to keep her composure. She was suddenly burning hot and fought the urge to fan herself with her wedding program.

"You're blushing!" Melody cupped a hand over Tara's rapidly heating cheek.

"Stop touching my face, you're embarrassing me."

"I live to embarrass you, darling, it's the only time we get to see a flush of color on those pretty cheeks. Don't worry, he's not even looking at you any more."

Tara let her eyes dart quickly back to where he had been standing, but he was gone.

"I should probably find my new husband before he gets too drunk and falls under a table somewhere. Want to join me?"

"In a little while." *Jesse had seen her.* She had to at least say hello or things would be even more awkward between them. But she needed time to gather her strength and put on a brave face.

She was painfully aware that despite her expensive haircut, designer suit and sparkling manicure she was just a wallflower at someone else's wedding. And her design business—which was just starting to blossom when she last saw Jesse in Vegas—had overexpanded, blown up and left her with a huge debt she had no idea how to pay.

Right now she just wanted to cry.

Melody had started to move away but she turned back and reached a hand out to touch Tara's arm.

"I'm am sorry, you know. I come off as a hard-nosed old harpy, but I know how much you were hoping for with Gordon. I never thought he was worth it, but I know that doesn't make it hurt any less."

Tara swallowed. "It's good that he cheated on me. Makes it easier to despise him."

"But eight years? That's a long time and a lot of dreams to say goodbye to."

"Yes." Tara paused, her fingers wrapping unconsciously around the empty space vacated by the engagement ring she'd waited so long for. "Saying goodbye to the dreams is the tough part."

She and Gordon weren't perfect for each other, never had been, but somehow Tara had convinced herself he was the ideal companion for her. He was charming, poised and quietly handsome. He'd been to the right schools, he knew the right people, and he said the right things often enough to keep her on the end of a leash for eight long years.

It was the dreams—of two healthy children, traditional Christmases in their big suburban house, the happy family spending summers at the beach— that had really sustained her through eight years of an empty relationship.

"You'll just have to transfer that weighty burden of dreams to a new love object."

"No thanks, I'm done with dreaming. I'm all practical realities from now on."

"Don't get so practical that you won't date anyone else. Your thirtieth birthday is coming up so you don't want to spend too much time moping. You don't look a day over twenty-five, but those eggs in your ovaries won't respond to anti-wrinkle cream."

"Thanks for reminding me." Her gut clenched. She hadn't told Melody that she already had reason to suspect that she was infertile.

"I don't want you to be so gun shy that you won't take a chance on someone new."

"I'm not much for taking chances anyway. And I don't want you setting me up on a lot of blind dates with your castoffs because you think my expiration date is approaching fast."

"Look at him now." Tara quickly pulled down Melody's pointing finger but her eyes found its target. There he was, his back to them, bending over a black dog that had wandered in from somewhere, ruffling the fur on its neck.

"Nice rear."

"Melody!"

"Well he does. I calls 'em as I sees 'em. Uh-oh, he's talking to the dog."

He murmured something and he took a morsel of food out of the napkin he was carrying and fed it to the fluffy mutt who wagged his tail in enthusiastic appreciation.

Tara could see his face in profile. It was a kind face, his strong features softened by a smile. He was kneeling and let the dog jump up to him and lick his cheek.

She realized that a smile had spread across her face and she quickly wiped it off before Melody could see it. An odd sensation had started way down inside her tummy. A tingling, stirring sensation that had nothing to do with her emotional response to the wedding and everything to do with her physical response to this man. She tried to tear her attention away, to look at anything else, the tent, the trees, the blinding sun.

But she couldn't take her eyes off him. And she was getting hot again.

He stood up and turned in their direction as he raised himself to his full height. Tara instinctively held her breath. Perspiration pricked at her armpits. He looked at her looking at him.

Melody smiled and sipped her champagne, Tara plastered on a polite grimace to hide whatever unidentifiable feelings were beginning to seize hold of her and heave her about like a bucket of water on a ship's deck.

He smiled, and those dark eyes rested on her for an instant, shooting a dart of something toward her that threatened to knock her off her feet.

Tara's heart began to pound. For one terrifying instant she thought he was going to walk over to them, but he didn't. He turned and went back inside the tent with his new friend at his heels. Tara heaved a mercifully inaudible sigh of relief. She even caught herself patting her hair, as if she'd just been caught in a tornado.

"I think he was putting on a show for you."

"What?"

"You know, letting you know that he's good with animals and children and all that. Showing you that he's kind, nurturing, just the man you need to help you heal the scars of a lost love and learn to live again."

"You're insane. I'm sure he hates me. I had sex with him then two days later I told him I was now engaged to someone else."

"Being unavailable just makes men more enthusiastic, darling. Sad but true. He's definitely carrying a torch for you. You're going home with him tonight."

"I most certainly am not. And I'm going to pour this champagne over you if you don't stop going on about him." She lifted her glass.

"Please don't! This dress will shrink to doll size if it comes in contact with moisture. Shame I won't shrink along with it. I can't help myself. You're too much fun to tease."

"I know. I'm prim and humorless. It's fun to make jokes about me because I'll never get them anyway."

"Did Gordon tell you that?"

"It was implied rather than stated."

"That arrogant prick. Well, we'll show him. You're going to come inside with me and find my sweet new husband and we're going to have a gay old time and word will get back to Gordon just how little you need him."

"And about how I couldn't find a date to bring with me."

"Who cares? All the better to meet available single men. You don't want to be tied down with a courtesy date when something much more promising is waiting for you at the buffet. Come on!"

They headed inside the tent and picked up plates, then Melody got pulled away into another conversation. Tara helped herself to a lobster tail and some three-bean salad, though she had no appetite at all. She was just wondering if she should go out and hide behind a tree, when Melody grabbed her arm and assaulted her with a loud stage whisper. "Come on, I've got him cornered for you."

"Oh, Melody, I can't. I'm just not…"

"Nonsense, come on before I make a scene." Melody locked her arm firmly around Tara's, which almost tipped the lobster tail onto the ground, then dragged her across the big tent toward a group of people standing near the bar.

Her chest tightened as they walked closer. Jesse was half turned away from her and couldn't see her but suddenly it seemed like all the rest of the room had shifted into black and white and he was in color, a little bit larger than life, his empty drinking glass tilted sideways as he lifted his arm to scratch his wrist inside the cuff of his shirt.

"It's a lovely wedding," said someone to Melody.

"Yes, you got real lucky with the weather," said another random stranger. "It's not usually this warm after Thanksgiving." Tara stood there, painfully aware of Jesse while Melody made small talk with someone for what seemed like an eternity but was probably only a few seconds. Jesse stood less than ten feet away, but still hadn't seen them.

You can do this. Just be polite and make your escape. He probably barely remembers you.

"Jesse, darling," Melody's voice boomed in her ear. "Look who I found."

He turned. She swallowed hard.

"Hi, Tara." He held out a big hand and she had no choice but to shake it.

Something mischievous danced in his dark eyes, which looked intently at her. His hand was burning hot, or was that her hand? He pressed her palm to his gently but firmly.

"Hello," she replied, willing herself to sound casual while blood pumped audibly inside her head. He held her hand and her gaze, looking into her eyes as if he was searching for something.

The way he held her hand, just staring at her as if they were alone together, steamed up her body and fogged up her brain in a way that made her incapable of polite speech. Her palm began to sweat and she tried to pull it back, but he tightened his powerful fingers around it and held it a little longer than decency called for before releasing it.

Tara felt the heat of a blush rising above the neckline of her dress and up past the string of pearls around her neck. Jesse smiled, still looking at her. She racked her brain for something to say to break the awful tension of the silence that thundered between them.

"Jesse," said Melody, extending a diamond-and-pearl-encrusted arm toward him. Tara prayed that Melody wasn't going to say anything to humiliate her. "You remember that Tara's an interior designer."

"Of course." Jesse smiled politely. "That's why you were in Vegas the year I won the bull riding finals."

"Exactly. So I maybe Tara could help you decorate the new guest quarters you're building at your ranch. I know you were probably thinking you'd slap up some striped wallpaper and plaid curtains and a few eighteenth century horse prints, but Tara will create an environment that will make your clients stay longer and spend more. Psychology 101, make them feel entitled to the best."

"Striped wallpaper and plaid curtains?" Jesse raised an eyebrow at Melody. "I was just going to paint the walls white and throw some bedspreads on the beds."

"Then you can see how much you need Tara to set you on the right path."

Jesse looked at Tara. "It's good to see you again." His deep voice rang bells inside her that had been silent for years.

She nodded, still unable to think of a complete sentence that made any sense. His dark eyes seemed to see right through her, past her carefully coiffed facade, to the loneliness and turmoil within. "Yes," she finally managed. "How are you?"

"Pretty good. I've spent the last two years building out my ranch. I train horses and host the occasional dude ranch weekend. It turns out I have more people wanting to come than I had rooms to accommodate them, so I've built some new guest cottages. I could use a hand fixing them up."

Tara nodded, trying to keep a straight face as the curve of his lips caused a disturbing fluttering sensation in the pit of her stomach. It sounded like he wanted her to show up with a paintbrush and a can-do attitude. "I do design interiors for new construction, and I have a team of trusted subcontractors who can do all the work of implementing them."

"I know." His half smile broadened. "Melody's told me all about it."

"Seriously, you two should talk," said Melody. "Exchange cards or something, Tara will give your rooms what it takes to stand apart from the crowd."

Thanks mom, thought Tara. How embarrassing, having herself thrust upon a man she'd coolly rejected just two years ago.

Jesse was still looking at her, smiling, as if they had all the time in the world and no one was watching. She covered her confusion by fumbling in the tiny bag slung over her shoulder. She always carried a few cards with her as you never knew when a potential client might materialize.

She offered him the card and he took it between two bronzed fingers. She noticed that his nails were a little dirty. Which was probably pretty typical of a cowboy who lived on a working ranch. She didn't know anything about horses. She and Jesse had literally nothing in common, except that they'd gone to school together a million years ago in a different lifetime. And had blistering chemistry that short-circuited her common sense.

That night in Vegas had been a crazy, foolish mistake.

"I don't have a card myself, but I'll be sure to keep yours in a safe place." His hand reached under his tuxedo jacket and tucked it into his jeans.

Tara searched her brain for something to say but came up empty again, which was pretty sad for someone whose career depended on sweet talking people into spending money.

"The cottages are pretty simple," Jesse offered, filling the gaping hole in their conversation. "Just somewhere to spend the night while I'm giving a seminar or showing them some horses for sale."

"What kind of seminars do you teach?" Phew, she still had a few working brain cells left.

"Different aspects of horsemanship, how to relate better to your horse, solving behavioral problems, that sort of thing."

"Where is your ranch?" Another perfectly appropriate question. She was almost having a normal conversation now. If she could just stop that pounding in her head she'd be fine. She couldn't help but notice that here was still no wedding ring on the broad hand that rubbed over his clean-shaven chin.

"East of the city, just over an hour, depending on traffic. I hope that's not too far out of your range."

"That's fine."

"Hello Tara, long time no see." Tara turned to see Bowie, Jesse's brother, who she'd met the year Jesse won the rodeo finals.

"Hi Bowie." She kissed him on each cheek. "Congratulations. I heard you won the bull riding finals this year." She'd kept up with news of the circuit since watching the brothers ride two years ago.

"Yep. Finally pulled it off." Tall, tanned and rugged, just like his brother, Bowie had fairer hair and a mischievous gleam to his green eyes.

"Are you quitting the circuit like Jesse did, or are you going to keep riding bulls?"

"I'm putting myself out to pasture." He squeezed the pretty brunette standing next to him. "I've met the love of my life and we're going to run our ranch together." He kissed her on the cheek. "This is Lucy Neel. Soon to be Lucy West."

Lucy thrust out a hand and Tara shook it. "Congratulations to both of you. That's wonderful." Lucy glowed with happiness that warmed even Tara's bruised heart.

Bowie already had a more settled air about him. "We'll have to have you and Melody out to visit our new place once it's up and running. We're just drawing up plans for our house. We might need your professional expertise once the walls and windows are up."

"I'd love that," she fibbed. The last thing she needed was to spend a lot of time around Jesse's extended family. So his wild, playboy younger brother was now ready to marry and settle down. Apparently everyone around here was about to enjoy married bliss except her.

"They're expecting a baby," said Jesse. "So they're trying to get the house up and running in a hurry."

"Wow. That's great." Tara tried to sound pleased while the hole in her own heart opened just a little wider. "I'm thrilled for you."

"We're building our house big enough to accommodate a good sized family," said Bowie with a grin. "So I'm pretty sure we'll need some help making the place look good. Especially since we have our hands full with the animals. I'm bringing my bulls over from Jesse's place, and Lucy already runs a big horse boarding operation."

"So you can see that the West family is in dire need of your professional skills," said Jesse.

"I'd be happy to help." Now she was lying through her teeth. If she didn't get out of here pretty quick she was going to cry in front of everyone. "Um, I've got to get going. I have to make a phone call. You have my card."

Jesse's raised one eyebrow slightly. "I'll give you a call during the week, then."

She nodded. "Great." His unwavering gaze was making her very uncomfortable.

"Bye, Tara, it was nice to see you again."

She did her best to nod politely, her mouth devoid of sensible words to say, then turned to make a break for it.

Phew! She'd managed to negotiate the encounter with Jesse without undue humiliation. Her head still throbbed, too much champagne probably, and she could feel sweat trickling down inside her dress. Jesse West had her thoroughly rattled.

Tara thought suddenly of her card in his pocket, nestled snugly against his big thigh. Would he call? Maybe he'd take pleasure in coolly ignoring her. She certainly deserved it after the way she'd treated him two years ago.

"I've got a bit of a headache," she said to Melody who had followed her outside. "Would you be mortally offended if I took off?"

"Fine with me. Today's mission has been

accomplished. I got married and you have a date."

"He probably won't call."

"Of course he'll call!

"I really don't want him to." Not that she was in any position to turn down paying work. If he called, she'd pretty much have to jump on it. "Oh, Melody, why can't you just let me be?"

"Perfect and perfectly unhappy?"

"I'm not all that unhappy. I've hit a bump in the road and I'm going to drive right over it and keep on going. You'd better go find your husband." And she swept away before Melody could assault her with any more bad advice.

Once back in her car and safely off the expensive rented estate, Tara battled a tremendous urge to light a cigarette. She had quit nearly four weeks ago, the same day that Gordon had told her his wonderful news: he'd been cheating on her, and his girlfriend was pregnant.

She'd only taken up smoking anyway because of Gordon. He was a smoker himself and had enjoyed company in his after-dinner vice. The next thing she knew she had a ten-a-day habit.

Well, darn it, she wasn't going to give him the satisfaction. Gordon-free and smoke-free, that was the new Tara Kent, and she had an urgent appointment with a hot bath and an even hotter cup of tea.

She didn't even have time to get in her bath before he called her and made an appointment for the following day.

2

Jesse West's ranch was pretty far off the beaten path, and Tara was just beginning to wonder if she'd ever see civilization again when she spotted the words Singing Pines Ranch crudely printed on the battered mailbox.

She entered the unpaved driveway and followed it until shady oak woods parted to reveal a vista of open green fields crisscrossed with black post and board fencing. A large wood and stone barn dominated the ranch, and off to one side she could see a pretty farmhouse with a wraparound porch. Several smaller structures, new metal roofs gleaming in the sun, must be the guesthouses she was here to decorate.

She pulled into the parking area in front of the barn and parked next to three other cars. Jesse had told her to come to his office on the first floor of the barn, but as she opened her car door he emerged from the doorway and walked toward her.

Unfortunately he looked more gorgeous than ever in a dark gray plaid shirt and faded jeans. He offered a hand to help her out of her car, and she took it because it would have been rude to refuse. And the fact was she could use a hand. She wasn't sure why she had chosen to drive her Porsche today rather than the Suburban, but getting out of it was always a little like extracting crabmeat from a shell.

"Nice car."

"Thanks." That was why she'd driven the Porsche. It never failed to impress male clients. She'd worn low-heeled boots, in preparation for rustic footing, which made him seem even taller than she'd remembered.

Jesse smiled at her, and his smile caused a little tremor of nerves deep inside her. It was a friendly smile on the face of it, but something like mischief sparkled in those penetrating dark brown eyes.

Business, you're here on business. She retrieved her portfolio from the passenger side and slammed the door.

"You really should get a sign for the end of the driveway, something that will give your entrance some presence. Maybe a big sign suspended right over the driveway."

Amusement glimmered in his eyes. "I don't know. I don't like strangers snooping around. I don't want every Tom, Dick and Harry seeing my sign and thinking they'll drive up and check the place out. This is a very exclusive joint, you know."

"By appointment only?"

"Absolutely. I just wish it hadn't taken so long to get an appointment with you. It's been more than two years since I last saw you."

She swallowed. She'd had a wild fling with him. Then told him it was over. "I did explain what happened."

His eyes darkened slightly. "You got back together with your ex."

"We'd only been broken up a short time before I

went to Vegas. I'd been with him for six years. He finally proposed." She didn't want him to think she was an idiot. Even though she was.

"So you disappeared right out of my life for the second time, leaving me to nurse a broken heart."

She tried for a slight smile. "I hope it healed."

"My heart? Yes, it healed up just fine. A little scar tissue but that's made it tougher in the long run." He smiled and Tara felt a low rumble of something starting deep inside her. Then he glanced at her ring finger.

She fought an urge to shove her embarrassingly ringless hand into her pocket. *Back to business.* "Do you want to start by showing me the rooms you're looking to decorate, or should I get a feel for the place by looking at the barn first?"

"Since we're here, I'll show you around the barn. Come on in." He led the way back into the dark doorway. "The horses are all out grazing right now, but this where I bring clients to look at a prospect."

He led her through the barn aisle, and Tara was impressed by the polished wood and beautiful painted wrought iron bars of the stalls, obviously custom crafted, which gave the barn interior a nineteenth-century flair. The rich smell of hay and horses was inviting rather than acrid.

"Very nice."

"Thanks." Jesse smiled, obviously proud of his barn. There was a bucket lying on its side in the barn aisle and Jesse bent over to pick it up. As he reached forward, Tara found her eyes suddenly planted on the taut denim stretched over his firm backside.

Good lord, he had a body. His thighs were broad and powerful, flexing as he bent to retrieve the bucket. His shoulders, too, and her eyes flashed over his thick brown forearm as he lifted the bucket and turned toward her.

"Can't have buckets lying around when we have a special guest visiting."

Tara was temporarily deprived of speech, her mind still reeling from its crude appraisal of Jesse West's physique. What on earth had come over her? She wasn't one to drool over a man's body like a gawker at an all-male strip show.

She usually wasn't even attracted to big muscular guys. She preferred a more understated type of male. Someone whose power came from the way he commanded a particular turn of phrase, not how well he could handle a thousand-pound horse. Someone who wielded a pen rather than a coiled leather whip like the one she could see mounted on the wall at the end of the aisle.

Jesse put the bucket down outside the stall and led the way down the aisle toward his office. It was basic and utilitarian, a big room with off-white walls and a neat desk. Shelves of trophies lined one wall, and photographs of horses in simple black frames another. The whole effect was simple, masculine, appealing.

"So you think I need some striped wallpaper and plaid curtains in here?"

"Definitely not." Tara was glad to have a reason to smile at him. "I like it. You might want to think about taking the walls a couple of shades darker, perhaps going with a hint of color, something natural, a sage green or a warm gray. That would create a bit more atmosphere."

Jesse nodded, "Sounds good to me."

"Are these all awards you have won?" She gestured to the impressive array of trophies.

"Not me so much as my horses."

"I bet you deserve as much credit as them." He was clearly as successful with horses as he was at bull riding. He'd won the world bull riding championship during their whirlwind affair. And he'd been the shy kid who got picked on in high school.

She'd once been known as Princess Tara and voted Most Likely to Succeed. And look where they both were now. She was being sued for her last dime, and he was decorating expensive guesthouses at his vast ranch.

He gestured to a framed photograph. She had a hard time tearing her eyes from his strong, tanned hand to look at the glossy picture. "This is Dante, the first horse I ever trained. I bought him from a dealer who said he was too spooky to ever amount to anything. Steadiest mount I own now. I still have him, he's semiretired, but he's been my best friend all these years."

The horse was black and looked pretty much like every other horse to Tara. She'd managed to skip right over that adolescent horse phase that most girls go through. One more reason they had almost nothing in common. "You should put up some Christmas decorations in here. Just something simple, a wreath, some natural pine boughs. I can arrange it if you like."

"That would be nice. We've been so busy I forget what time of year it is."

She certainly couldn't forget that it would soon be Christmas and she was probably going to be spending it by herself. Even her mom had booked a trip to visit a friend in Arizona. She couldn't face telling anyone about her lonely predicament, so she'd probably just pick at a stuffed turkey breast by herself on Christmas day. "Perhaps we should take a look at the rooms you want me to decorate."

"Sure, follow me." He exited the office through a door that opened directly to the outside and led her along a broad gravel path toward the new buildings.

The ranch was well manicured, the grass neatly trimmed, all the fences freshly painted, the paths edged with rows of stone block. The whole scene said, "Money, and lots of it."

They took a peek inside the six older guesthouses with stucco exteriors that he'd put up when he first built the ranch. The interiors looked like a chain hotel. No wonder he needed her. The new guesthouses were a step up—clad with local stone, and Tara approved of the carved custom moldings and elegant window trim.

"Each guesthouse has a bedroom with an adjoining bathroom and a small sitting room."

"Could you give me a brief profile of your clients, so I have some idea who we're dealing with?"

Jesse smiled at her. "You take your business very seriously, don't you?"

Was he laughing at her? "You don't get far in this market unless you take business seriously. I'm sure you know that."

"Do you make a real living picking out people's rugs and drapes?" He raised an eyebrow.

"I make a very good living, as it happens." She heard the edge of indignation in her voice and vowed to keep it under control. She'd been in Vegas to pitch for a huge commission when they'd last met. The money from that had sustained her for a solid year.

There was no reason for him to know that one of Gordon's cronies had convinced her to start her own line of specialty paints and she'd gotten into huge debt manufacturing the paints and all the marketing materials, then the distribution deal he'd promised had fallen through. She still owed the paint manufacturer fifty thousand dollars, and they were suing her for it.

"I used to think interior decoration was one of those occupations for bored housewives." Jesse led the way into the sitting room, which was centered comfortably around a big stone fireplace. "I'm glad you set me straight."

She cast a sideways glance at him. He was mocking her. By now he already knew she'd devoted most of her adult life to pursuing a position as the spouse of Gordon Van Zant. No doubt he thought it was hilarious that she'd thrown him over—twice—and wasted so much effort for nothing.

No doubt he had every right to be mad at her.

But he didn't look mad. He looked curious. His gaze wandered slowly over her conservative pantsuit, down to her new calfskin boots, heating her skin as it moved. She felt like a horse he was appraising.

She turned quickly toward the fireplace and ran a finger over the cherry wood of the fireplace surround. "The wood is attractive, but I think a pale chalk paint would complement the stone and fit the rustic character of the building better."

"He wasn't good enough for you." He spoke slowly, his voice low.

"Excuse me?" She heard her voice rising, and she struggled to keep her temper under control.

"I know you didn't get married."

She cursed Melody, who'd probably told him the whole sob story. She turned to face him, and his dark eyes flashed. His gaze seared into her, right past her carefully manicured facade to the lonely, scared woman beneath. "Melody told you."

"Nope. I can just tell."

How embarrassing. Did she have *failure* written all over her despite her efforts to look chic and confident? "How?" She turned away from him and opened the glass doors to the fireplace, peering inside in an attempt to distract herself and hide the color spreading over her face.

"I can read people, just like I can read horses."

"You can read minds?" She still didn't turn and look at him. Her hair stood on end as she contemplated the terrifying prospect that he might be able to read her mind, which had been barreling out of control ever since she came into contact with Jesse West.

"No, I can't read minds. I can read bodies, body language."

"But you can tell what people are thinking?" She couldn't hide the edge of trepidation in her voice.

"Sometimes." His dark unreadable eyes grazed her face. "But mostly I can tell what they're feeling."

"So what am I feeling right now?" She didn't even know what she was feeling so she'd be damned if he did.

3

Amusement glinted in Jesse's eyes. "You're mad at me. You want to run for your Porsche and drive out of here as fast as possible. Failing that you'd like to deck me."

Tara knew her face was blazing. He was toying with her, and likely she deserved it. Maybe she should run for her car while the getting was good. But he'd surely take that as a sign of weakness. She was no quitter.

"I most certainly am not. Why would I be mad? I'm wondering why we're wasting valuable time chitchatting about body language when I'm here to decorate your guest cottages."

Jesse chuckled, looking right at her—laughing at her. She felt her eyes widen. What the heck was he doing to her? Why was she getting so riled up?

"Go on, take your best shot. I'd like to see pretty Princess Tara in a passion over me."

"Don't call me that." Had he brought her here to get revenge on her? If he kept on like this who knows, she might deck him. Gordon had left her with enough pent-up rage to fuel a WWF match, so if that got unleashed, anything was possible.

"Listen, I'm a busy woman, though apparently it

gives you pleasure to think of me as some kind of bored housewife without a husband. I've got work to do, so if you're not serious about decorating this place let's just shake hands and call it a day, shall we?"

He nodded, still smiling that infuriating smile. "All right, Princess Tara." The old nickname—that she'd once laughingly mocked but secretly loved—tugged at an uncomfortable place inside her. "Lets talk carpets and curtains."

Tara took another deep breath to clear her mind and focus on what she did well. "You still haven't told me who your clients are, men, women, age group?"

"Rich people, a mix of men and women, mostly between thirty and fifty. Like you and me I guess." He shrugged. The smirk was gone from his face, and his features were softened by an oddly tender expression that took Tara by surprise. It reminded her for a moment of the shy boy she'd befriended in high school.

Pulse pounding, she dragged her attention back to the room and the task at hand. "Rustic but sophisticated is probably the way to go. Soft grays, some blue accents. I can source some vintage items as accessories."

"I never found anyone good enough either."

His confession came right out of the blue. And the way Jesse said it, his voice soft and reflective, made Tara's hot rage evaporate into the wood-dust-scented air. Maybe he had a right to be a little angry with her, to hold a grudge for how she had treated him. There probably was a better way to end an affair than a terse phone call saying that you hoped what happened in Vegas stayed in Vegas.

But it didn't make sense to apologize now. It was

all water under the bridge. There she went with the clichés again. They were so reassuring when you suddenly lost all faith in your own judgment.

She glanced at the stone tile floor. "An area rug would add warmth and create a focal point. Easy to clean, too."

"Practical."

"Yes." He looked like he was actually paying attention to her decorating advice. "White-painted wood blinds—or perhaps interior shutters. And some horse-related paintings and prints. I have a contact in New York who goes to auctions there for me."

"Real antiques?"

"Yes, if you like."

"I think I do like. It sounds pretty classy." She glanced at him and he didn't seem to be mocking her, so she went on.

"I think the fireplace should be painted white or off-white, and the trim around the windows, too. That's important to a period look; they never left wood unpainted in the old days if they could afford to paint it."

"Are we trying to re-create the old days?"

Tara detected a distinct hint of double entendre in his words, and she felt her back stiffen.

"We don't have to. If you prefer stained wood we can work that into the decor. A lot of my clients feel that way nowadays. If they've paid for real wood, they want people to see it."

"I like the rich color of the wood, the grain, the imperfections that make each piece unique. It seems a shame to cover it up." Jesse paused, studying her with those dark eyes again. Then he spoke slowly. "Maybe people didn't always know what they were doing in the old days."

Maybe they didn't. Covering up the grain, hiding her imperfections, was that what Tara had been doing when she shut Jesse out of her life? The night before she left boarding school for good, she'd stayed up late telling him the disastrous news about her parents' divorce. He'd seen her at her weakest and hadn't been afraid. She'd never shared her thoughts and feelings with anyone like that again.

Jesse was the only person who'd seen her unvarnished, laid bare, and he had never tried to use it against her until now.

Jesse was looking at her calmly but without a hint of hostility. He couldn't read her mind, but she knew he could tell what she was thinking.

"People like to look back and wax all nostalgic about the old days," he said. "Myself I'd rather live in the present. The old days weren't always so great."

"I agree. No running water, no central heating, no indoor toilets."

"I spent enough time managing without indoor toilets on the rodeo circuit. Some of the smaller shows I did to get points when I was first starting out didn't even have port-a-potties. You had to sneak off into the woods." Jesse wiped the smile off his face and shook his head. "Gosh, I'm being crude. I'm sorry. I'm sure you're not in the least bit interested."

What the heck was he doing ranting about peeing in the woods? Here he was, finally alone with the one woman in the world who'd fascinated him more than any other, and he's talking about pissing outside? Very refined, Jesse, no wonder she keeps ditching you.

God, she was beautiful. Those forget-me-not blue

eyes still clear and bright, sparkling windows on her bright soul. She didn't look a day older, just more elegant, womanly, lovelier than ever.

Don't smile! You don't want her to know what you're thinking, you idiot.

He let his eyes follow her as she walked to the far side of the room and bent down to examine the moldings around the floor. What a sweet ass.

And she didn't marry the guy. He was willing to bet that she wasn't even dating someone. She had that edge of insecurity that you mostly saw on people who didn't have anyone to go home to at night. Or who went home to the wrong person.

He probably had it himself, though he was pretty sure it didn't show. He'd had women all right, a lot of them, over the years, but never this one. Not for more than one night, anyway. And looking at her now, he could see that she'd always been the one he wanted to come home to.

Don't even think it!

Damn, but his mind had a way of running away with him. That night in Vegas had rekindled the old fires deep inside him, and he hadn't managed to put them out properly since. Lucky thing he was such a student of body language. He knew how to control his so that no one knew what was going on in his mind unless he wanted them to. Now if only he could get control over his thoughts he'd really be in business.

Tara straightened up quickly. She probably thought he was laughing at the sight of her bent double over the woodwork.

"It is cherry isn't it?"

"Should be, unless the contractor cheated me."

Now some men might see a crude joke in the cherry thing, but fortunately he was still too much of a gentleman to go down that road.

He'd spent too much time traveling on the rodeo circuit with his brother Bowie. And now even his wild young brother had settled down and was starting a family.

He let a smile wander across his face. Yes, sometimes the right woman was just what it took to turn an overgrown boy into a man.

"The woodwork is beautiful. I'm with you, let's leave it unpainted and choose a wall color that contrasts nicely."

"A creative blending of the past and the present."

"Exactly." She ignored his little reference to the "past" and smiled at him, and he saw that she'd regained her composure. He was glad. He hadn't meant to provoke her like that. He hadn't been able to help himself though. He could see past that pretty picture she painted. He'd seen past it before, that one night when she'd let him get close to her. He'd finally kissed her, then she'd vanished and left him with nothing but memories and longing.

He knew that she was hurting again.

She was thirty—or close—and had never been married. If there'd been any competition for "girl most likely to be happily married to Mr. Right within five years of high school" she would probably have won it. Funny how things turned out.

"Shall we take a look at the bedroom?"

"Sure. This way." He gestured for her to leave the room first and head up the stairs. This cottage was on two small floors, the bedroom directly over the living room, with a balcony above the front porch.

"Were you thinking of carpet for the stairs?" Tara asked, as she climbed the stairs in front of him.

"So people can go sneaking up and down them late at night without clunky footfalls giving them away?"

She had reached the top of the stairs, and he was sad to see the enchanting view of her rear end mounting them turn out of sight. He raised an eyebrow as she turned to look at him, and she gave him a withering glance that tickled him in the most pleasurable way.

"That wasn't exactly what I had in mind. The wide oak boards are lovely. I think it would be a shame to cover them up."

"They were taken from an old barn up in Maine somewhere. I had them sanded down and refinished." He was glad she'd noticed the flooring. He noticed the way things looked, and he knew what he liked. She bent down to touch the smooth wood, and his heart thumped uncomfortably in his chest at the sight of her suit pants stretching over those long, slender legs.

"It was worth the trouble; they really add character to the space. I wouldn't have thought those kinds of period details were your cup of tea."

She stood up and looked at him. Her back was straight, her eyes challenging. But he could see that she was wary, defensive, a little afraid of what he would say to her. And he couldn't deny that he liked having the upper hand for once.

"I don't think you know too much about my cup of tea." Lord knows what she thought of him, but he was beginning to hope he'd get the chance to shatter a few more of her assumptions.

"I'm good at guessing how people like their tea, actually."

"Oh, yeah?"

She was smiling, looking relaxed. So she was going to try to read his mind, was she?

"You like your tea strong but milky and with lots of sugar."

Damn! How did she know that?

"How do you know I don't like it black, with a slice of lemon?"

"I can just tell, that's all. Am I right?"

Jesse felt his face crack into a grin. "Yeah, three teaspoons, and cream if you've got it. Pretty disgusting, huh?"

She shrugged and smiled. He was glad she had his number on something. Against his better judgment he liked her. He'd always liked her. But that didn't mean he didn't want to get a little revenge while he had her within reach.

Jesse opened the door to the bedroom. A newly delivered bed made of weathered pine, complete with plastic-covered mattress, stood in the center of the room.

"Jumping the gun a little by ordering furniture before you've painted, weren't you?"

"Bed's the most important thing," he jumped onto it and stretched out full length on his back. "You've got to start with the most important thing. Besides, when I'm lying on the bed I can appreciate the view out the window from this angle." He directed his eyes toward the large multipaned windows.

"Come on in, you need to get a feel for the atmosphere from up here." He patted the crinkly plastic next to him with one of those long-fingered brown hands.

To her chagrin Tara found her errant mind wondering what it would be like to bounce onto the bed next to Jesse West's big body. The mattress looked a little soft the way the bulk of him made a dent in it. Anyone lying next to him would probably roll toward him.

They'd end up pressed against that chest, making wrinkles in his soft gray shirt, jostling against the coarse denim that covered his powerful thighs.

She was growing hot and flustered again. Her mom had started menopause early. That could explain the hot flashes she seemed to be experiencing this morning, as well as her inability to get pregnant. She'd quit smoking and drinking and tried pretty hard to get pregnant that first year back with Gordon. No luck. Then he'd insisted that she stop trying until they were married.

Which obviously didn't happen.

The urge for a cigarette was becoming overwhelming. Maybe she needed that silly-looking patch after all. She moved over to the window and looked out. She could see horses grazing in the well-manicured pastures and a man with a weed trimmer mowing the edge of the driveway.

She sensed Jesse's eyes burning into her backside. Probably noticing how much wider it had grown. Not surprising, since she'd come dangerously close to attempting death-by-chocolate in the weeks since Gordon dumped her. She was getting older, she was alone, she was all on edge, her hormones were running amok, and she wasn't sure how much longer she could hold it all together.

"You don't want to come into my bed with me, Princess Tara?"

He said it softly, and oddly it didn't make her hackles rise the way she would have hoped. It made something altogether different rise, an uneasy feeling in the pit of her stomach, an odd tugging sensation that she couldn't identify and didn't like one bit.

She knew that if she turned to look at him that smirk on his face would fill her with righteous indignation. But when she did she was taken aback to see him not smiling at all.

"You've changed a lot, Jesse West. You used to be polite." She was only half joking.

"To a fault. Look how far my politeness got me."

Touché. If he hadn't been such a gentleman she wouldn't have been able to cast him off so easily.

"I'm not so polite any more. Not so nice either." He stretched out on the bed, arms crossed behind his head. He looked very relaxed and at ease, and that made Tara feel less so.

"I've noticed."

"If you're too nice people don't respect you. But then you'd know about that, wouldn't you? You always knew how to be nice but not too nice."

"I have no idea what you mean." She generally tried to be pleasant and accommodating, though it was true, she didn't let people use her. You didn't last long in business if you let people walk all over you.

She'd let Gordon walk all over her though. She was covered with his footprints from head to toe. He'd taken what he wanted when he wanted it, then he'd sauntered casually away, taking her hopes for the future with him. A shadow must have passed over her face because she glanced at Jesse and saw him frown.

"Someone's hurt you, Princess Tara."

"Don't call me that." She said it half-heartedly, a reflex. Hearing him say her name, her old nickname, touched something inside her. It touched something soft, defenseless and painfully sensitive. And it hurt, she hurt, she just hurt all over.

Jesse scooted to the foot of the bed and hopped onto the floor. He put an arm around her. She knew she should try to push him away, but at that instant she didn't have the strength. She wanted a cigarette. She wanted to lie down. She wanted her dreams back.

He wrapped his arms around her and she felt the last shreds of her dignity abandon her as she began to sob softly. Jesse held her, rubbing her back gently with his hand.

She had no idea what she was doing. The tears kept on flowing, and it was a blessed relief to let them come. She'd been holding so much so close to her chest for so long.

She buried her face in Jesse's collar and let the warmth of him soothe her as her body shook slightly with the uncontrolled movements of her diaphragm. She could barely feel her legs, but she let his strong arms hold her up. She must really have gone crazy now.

The scent of Jesse, musky maleness with a sweet undertone like honey or molasses, revived her like smelling salts. Gradually, she found herself blinking back the tears, gasping for her breath, wondering what she was going to say now.

"I—"

"Don't talk."

Something buzzed and hummed in the air between them. Jesse pulled his head back just enough to look at her, and the wary, tender look in his eyes pulled out the last pin that was holding her together. The hypnotic thrumming echoed in her blood as the distance between them collapsed to nothing, and their lips met, hot, open, each mouth willing the other to plunge in and get warm.

A stinging heat wave rose through her body as her tongue streaked out of her mouth into Jesse's. She pulled him close to her, hungrily drinking in the taste of the man who unraveled her in a way no one else could.

She wanted to lose herself in him. She wanted him to save her. For his powerful embrace to protect her, hold her up and rebuild her.

She pressed her body against his, craving the strength of every hard, masculine inch of it. He responded, hugging her tightly, sucking her mouth, eating her kisses.

His hands roved up and down her back, unleashing mini-cyclones of sensation inside her. She straddled one of his thighs, hard as steel between her shuddering legs, pulling herself against it. Their mouths were still fused together, their tongues licking, tasting, fighting, dancing.

Her hand reached down to his waist and pulled his shirt up, wanting to touch the hot skin beneath. She pressed her fingers against the base of his spine, still kissing him with the force of every nerve and muscle in her body, and pushed her hands down inside his jeans, cupping his buttock with eager fingers.

She could feel his erection pressing against the front of his jeans as he gloried in the sensations she was creating in him. She heard him moan, a deep guttural groan, though their mouths didn't part even for a fraction of a second. She still tasted him, hot, metallic, his saliva mingling with hers in a powerful brew that made her drunk on him.

She pressed her breasts against his chest. They were alive with sensation, plump with excitement, and feeling it he rubbed them with his hand, hardening her nipples and making her gasp, a breath lost into the heat of his mouth. Everything inside her body felt like it was about to explode, to come bursting out, to splash a wild rainbow of color across the white walls of the empty room.

"Jesse! Are you up there? Someone is trespassing along the eastern border. A blue truck." Unwelcome sound penetrated the clamoring crescendo of the blood inside her head as a male voice called up the stairs followed by a rhythmic thudding of footsteps. "Jesse!"

"Damn." Wild-eyed, Jesse pulled back from her and Tara staggered backward across the room. Reeling, literally giddy with lust, she pressed a hand to her mouth, trying to regain some composure. She had no idea what had happened to her, and the room was still spinning as a man entered.

The man looked from Jesse to her and an odd expression crossed his face.

"Sorry to interrupt, but you said to be sure to report any strange activity. They're driving right along the fence line on your land."

"Thanks, Manny. I'll be right down." Manny tactfully disappeared.

Tara turned away from Jesse and tried to smooth her hair. Her wits were returning to her, and she did not like what they were telling her. Ancient history had just repeated itself—she'd cried and he'd kissed her—but in a way that would have shocked and scandalized prim young Princess Tara.

The horror of what had happened flooded her brain, and she decided that since decorum had already gone to hell in a handbasket she might as well go with her instincts and run.

She shot past Jesse and was down the stairs and out the door in one white-hot second. She heard his footsteps behind her, but she flashed across the gravel driveway, sprinting in her new boots, the hot morning sun blinding her as she streaked toward her car.

Thank heavens she'd left the car unlocked, the keys in the glove compartment. She started the engine and gunned backward into the turnaround as Jesse came pounding down the path after her. She willed herself not to look at him as she spun her car around in a screech of flying gravel and sped off down the driveway toward the road.

Jesse West's words seeped back into the edges of her shattered consciousness. The words came slow, low, gently mocking: "I'd like to see pretty Princess Tara in a passion over me."

Well, she had certainly given him what he wanted, and he must be laughing himself reckless over it.

4

It wasn't until much later that day, after she'd been for a seven-mile run, eaten an entire box of artisanal cheese straws and resisted countless cigarettes, that she realized she'd left her portfolio at Jesse West's ranch.

She wasn't even sure where she'd put it down. She knew she had it with her in his office, and she thought she'd brought it over to the guesthouse. She'd probably put it on the floor when she was examining the woodwork.

Ugh. It wasn't exactly indispensable. She had some blueprints in it that belonged to one of her other clients and it would be embarrassing to say that she had lost them, but they could easily be replaced. She had some fabric swatches she could go back to the manufacturer for.

The leather portfolio itself was what she would be sad to part with. Her mom had bought it for her as a surprise when she had started her own business. It wasn't as if her mom were dead or anything, but it was a special gift that had always meant a lot to her. She knew her mom had been a little mystified, even disappointed by some of the choices she'd made in life, but she'd always been supportive.

Her mom was glad she'd broken up with Gordon. She'd never liked him.

Time for another hot bath. She turned on the faucets and lit a scented candle.

The phone rang and she picked it up.

"So how'd it go with Jesse?" It was Melody. Tara squeezed her eyes closed tight. She had been trying so hard not to think about Jesse, and now she was going to have to fabricate some elaborate lies about him.

"I don't think the project is going to work out."

"Why not?"

"We didn't really see eye to eye." *Especially during the part when our eyes were closed. And my hand was inside his pants, clutching his buttocks.* She squeezed her eyes shut a little tighter.

"He didn't like your ideas?"

"Or maybe I didn't like his."

"Did something happen?" Melody's voice rose into a familiar accusatory whine.

"No, nothing." *Unless you count the part where I was rubbing my body against him like an aroused bullfrog.*

"You're lying to me. You are the worst liar in the known world. You couldn't deceive a newborn baby. If you don't tell me what happened I'm going to come over there with a bottle of merlot and a box of eclairs and force it out of you."

"Aren't you on your honeymoon in Mexico?"

"Gareth has a plane, darling. I can be there in two hours. Dish."

"There's something about Jesse that sets my nerves on edge."

"That would be his gorgeous looks and easy cowboy charm." She could hear the smile in Melody's voice.

She stiffened. "I'm not a fan of the cowboy charm. Seriously, things are just weird. I should never have slept with him in Vegas. You talked me into that, and it was all wrong. Especially when I came back and got engaged to someone else. Things are totally awkward between us now. I think he hates me."

"What did he say?"

"It wasn't his words, so much as—" *Hate* was the wrong word. But there was something fierce, unfamiliar, a little dangerous that flared between them. "I don't know, but I think it's better if I don't see him again."

"Stop being so obtuse, Tara! From everything I've heard he sounds divine and you're saying you couldn't see eye to eye with him enough to decorate his guesthouse. You've worked with some of the most impossible people in Austin. It doesn't add up."

"Something about him sets my teeth on edge." Well, not really her teeth, more her nipples. Her nerves. "He kept calling me princess."

"You're kidding." Melody laughed so hard that she began to cough. "That is awful."

"Not really. Everyone used to call me Princess Tara in high school." Now she was defending him? And he'd never called her princess when they were younger. They'd been friends, sure, but he'd been shy and ultra respectful back then. Now? Nerve, arrogance, brash male assertiveness, disarming self-confidence—Jesse West had them all in spades.

"So he's calling you princess and getting under your skin, and suddenly you lose the ability to accessorize?"

"We argued about whether to paint the woodwork."

"Well, I can understand that. Unpainted woodwork is so vulgar." She could hear Melody laughing silently at her.

"Anyway, I don't think I'm going to do the job. I need to stay really focused on cultivating new clients now that you're busy being married and living in Vegas half the time. I don't have time to waste on someone who winds me up."

"He's wealthy, darling, and so is his whole family."

"There are plenty of well-heeled clients out there."

"Not nearly as good-looking as Jesse West."

"Melody! I've got to go. There's someone at the door. Bye."

Phew, her house was enormous. Jesse checked the address again to make sure he had the right place. Somehow this was not what he'd pictured as the kind of place Tara would live. He'd have thought a cottage with roses around the door would suit her better. Not this brick behemoth with a pedimented entryway and rows of privet balls flanking the door like green sentries.

Christmas wreaths extravagant enough for a large shopping mall ornamented each window and the front door. Even the mailbox was festooned with holly, mistletoe and gold and red swagging. The whole place was screaming something, and it wasn't just CHRISTMAS, it was something more…urgent and unsettling.

And there was a large for sale sign on the front lawn.

Jesse walked up the slate walkway carrying her leather case. He rang the doorbell and tapped his toe on the stone step as he waited for her to answer. He'd found her address online since it hadn't been on her card. She probably didn't want clients showing up and bothering her at home.

She certainly didn't want *him* showing up and bothering her at home. He didn't know what the hell had happened there this morning, but it obviously had her running scared. He was more than a little shaken by it himself.

He wished it hadn't happened that way. That she hadn't cried on him and they hadn't kissed. It was too much like old times—that night in high school when they'd finally shared the kiss he'd dreamed of—and that story didn't have a happy ending.

He didn't think *he'd* actually made her cry. Somebody else had planted the seeds of those tears, and he just had that knack for tapping the spring. Women didn't really like it when you saw them cry. Nobody liked it.

What the heck was taking her so long? Maybe she wasn't home. He checked his watch. Nearly six in the evening. Not a great time to show up. A bit too close to dinner for most people, but he'd had a busy afternoon and hadn't been able to get away before now.

And that kiss. Well, better not to think about the kiss. It was a reflex action after all. Seeking comfort, reaching out to someone, anyone. Just because he'd gotten all excited and emotional over it didn't mean that she felt the same way.

He hung his head and turned away from the door. In a lot of ways that quiet, polite, self-effacing Jesse he used to be was a superior person to the confident bastard he'd become now. When people treated you like an expert on something sooner or later you start believing your own headlines and crowing like a rooster when you should be listening and watching.

The door opened and he spun around. Instinctively he could tell she was going to slam it in his face so he wedged his boot in the door frame and the door smacked against the steel toe cap when it came at him.

"Tara."

For a moment he thought she was going to slam the door into his boot again, and keep slamming until she knocked him right out of there. But she didn't. That was encouraging.

"What do you want?" Her pretty face wrinkled into a frown.

"I came to return your case."

"Thanks." She reached out a hand to take it from him.

"And I wanted to apologize for being a jerk."

"Oh, is that what it was?" She placed her hands on her trim hips and glared at him. She was getting angry again, and this time it didn't give him any thrill of pleasure.

"I was so glad to see you again. I behaved like an ass. I'm sorry I made you cry."

"You didn't make me cry." She crossed her arms over her chest. She seemed to be waiting for him to say something.

"I know, someone else did, and that's none of my business. I'd really like you to decorate my guesthouses."

"I'm sorry, I can't do it. I'm too busy."

"You wouldn't even have to work with me. Manny, my ranch manager, could handle all the day-to-day stuff."

"Is he the one who brought the phone up?" She started laughing. Laughing was an improvement. "He caught us inflagrante, and you expect me to just chit chat about paint swatches with him as if nothing ever happened?"

"He didn't see anything." Not entirely true. Manny's raised eyebrows had provoked Jesse to tell him that he had the worst goddam timing in the entire history of the world. But they had left it at that.

She snorted and shook her head.

Suddenly a tremendous crash came from inside the house and Tara wheeled around. "What the…" The door at the top of the stairs had flung open and water came crashing out of the doorway and down the stairs toward them. Tara ran into the house and up the stairs two at a time, splashing through the cascading water. And Jesse ran after her.

They were both completely drenched. Tara had sponged most of the water off the bathroom floor and Jesse had mopped up the stairs and the woodwork in the hallway. The Aubusson rug from the foyer was draped over the banisters, still dripping a little.

"I guess after all the work you've done I should at least offer you a cup of coffee."

"I've been down on my hands and knees scrubbing your floors, and you think you're going to fob me off with a cup of coffee? No way." He was grinning. He looked so darned cheerful she just couldn't hate him right now.

He'd pitched in without even a word and turned a hellish all-night task into a half-hour mop-up job.

And he hadn't said anything about anyone being moronic enough to leave a bath running unattended.

"You still want me to decorate your guest houses."

"Yup, and I won't settle for anything less."

"I have a lot going on."

"You'll just have to fit me in."

"Fair enough." She smiled, reluctant but willing to do the job. "It would have been a real nightmare trying to clean this up by myself. I'm sorry you're all wet."

Jesse shrugged, still smiling. "It's okay. It's a warm night."

"Come on up. I think I've got some shorts and a T-shirt that will fit you."

Woof, woof! Jesse felt like an eager puppy climbing the stairs behind her. He didn't even care that he was probably going to be presented with her ex-boyfriend's clothing. She agreed to take him on again!

Well, not him, his guest houses, but that was okay. It was a start.

He certainly wasn't sorry that she was all wet. She was wearing capris and a T-shirt, and he couldn't help but notice that she'd neglected to wear a bra. The T-shirt wasn't exactly clinging to her, but it was damp enough to show him some outlines that set his imagination racing.

Her hair was pulled up in a sort of bun thing that showed off her pretty face, and the damp tendrils of hair falling out of it were about the most charming and lovely frame he could have imagined.

But he was going to keep his tongue in check and his hands to himself. He had a second chance to get to know the lovely woman his favorite girl had become, and he wasn't going to blow it this time.

"Wait here." She left him in the hallway while she went into a room—her bedroom probably. He didn't blame her for making him wait outside after his bad behavior lounging around on the bed that morning. He looked up and down the hallway. The doors to the other rooms were open, and he couldn't resist glancing into a couple of them.

What did one person need this many rooms for? Even if she'd been living with some guy, which he didn't like to think about one bit, then she'd hardly need the six or seven bedrooms he could see.

She emerged with some black athletic shorts and gray T-shirt.

"Did these belong to your ex?" Probably a stupid question but it just came out.

"No," she smiled. "They're mine, for those days when I've overindulged on the chocolate cheesecake."

"You'd have to eat a lot of chocolate cheesecake to fit into these."

"Yeah, but it could happen." She handed him the clothes, then stood there with her hands on her hips. The pressure of her hands pulled her T-shirt down and threw her nipples into high relief. Jesse felt a stirring in his wet jeans. *Down, boy!*

"You haven't gained a single ounce since high school."

"That's what you think!"

"That's what I know." He began to unbutton his wet shirt.

"You can go in there." She pushed open a door and flicked on the light. She stayed outside and he went in to change. The room was pale pink, with little pink roses painted around the ceiling. Instead of a bed there was a white crib, and a matching dresser and changing table. A little girl's room.

Good lord. Had she had a baby? Had a baby and lost it? His blood ran cold. The pictures on the walls, nursery rhyme scenes and an alphabet mural, mocked him. The little room frightened him, and he quickly stripped off his wet clothes and pulled on the dry ones. He may have kissed her—even made love to her—but he didn't know anything at all about what Tara had been through in the last few years.

"You look like you've seen a ghost!" said Tara as he emerged.

"That room, it's a baby's room. Did you have a baby?"

Shocking him, she laughed. "Oh, no. I just decorated it as a baby's room. This house has far more rooms than I could actually use, but being a decorator I couldn't possibly leave any of them bare. I did this one up as a little girl's room, and, come here," she beckoned him down the hallway, "and this one as a little boy's room. I used green rather than blue because blue is so cold. I photographed them and use them in my portfolio."

Jesse felt cold looking into the lovingly decorated space with its teddy-bear-cowboy wallpaper and lamps decorated with cutout stars. This was about the saddest thing he'd ever seen. She'd decorated the rooms for children she didn't have, that she probably should have had by now.

He turned to her, lord knows what expression he had on his face, but she was smiling, hands still on her hips.

"What's the matter?"

He just looked at her. All that loveliness, her sweet smile, her nice figure, her sharp mind, and she'd wasted all those years on some jerk who didn't appreciate her at all.

"Nothing," he shook his head. "I guess I'll get going now. You probably want to make your dinner or something." For a brief moment he dared to entertain the idea that she'd ask him to stay.

"Yes, I probably should. I don't think I need to see the rest of the guesthouses, unless they're very different from that first one. I'll be able to come up with some ideas and samples based on what I saw today."

"Okay, sounds good."

"I'll contact you when I have something to show you." She was leading the way down the stairs. She still had a girlish spring in her step and didn't look a day over twenty, even from behind. Especially from behind, he thought, grinning.

Tara put a lot of thought into planning the decor for the rooms. It was a no-brainer to give them a rustic, farmhouse flair—aged metals, worn wood, repurposed vintage items—that would give the rooms character.

She suspected that Jesse West would have a lot of repeat visitors, satisfied customers who would come back to buy another horse or attend another seminar. She decided to give each of the six guest houses a subtle theme, so that visitors could have a different experience each time they came or could decide which one was "their" room and request it whenever they came to stay.

She was armed with a sheaf of sketches as she

pulled slowly into Jesse's parking area for the second time, this time driving her matronly Suburban and hoping that no one would recognize her as the speed demon in the silver Porsche.

Jesse had been perfectly polite and gentlemanly on the phone. There had been no references to the unfortunate events of her last visit to the ranch, and she planned to try to pretend that it hadn't happened.

"Hi, Tara." Again he greeted her at the door. "Come on into the office."

He poured her a cup of coffee as she spread her sketches and samples out over his uncluttered desk. She glanced up at him as she prepared to begin her presentation, and for the first time that day their eyes met properly. His were nut brown, cheerful and sparkling with something that looked like hope.

Oh, dear. Something flared in her chest, a very uncomfortable and vulnerable feeling. She usually prided herself on her ability to control her emotions—how else had she managed all those years with Gordon—and she didn't like the way Jesse messed with that.

Deep breath. You're in control here. She was a talented interior designer, he didn't know anything about her recent business disaster or that she was about to lose her house, so there was no need to get rattled.

"Themes, a different one for each room, a slightly different period flavor to each one, nothing gimmicky or intrusive. The first would be French country, with cool gray tones, decorative signs and ironwork...." She described her ideas, and Jesse listened quietly, his hands wrapped around his coffee cup, those hopeful eyes drifting from her face to her hands and back again as she showed him colors and patterns.

As she kept talking he kept listening—and she began to get unsettled when he didn't say anything at all. It was unusual for a client not to exclaim in delight or shake their head in disagreement over at least one small detail.

He hadn't taken a single sip of his coffee, and his big hands were still wrapped around the mug. His shirtsleeves were rolled up, revealing brown forearms, which rested on the desk. His face was very clean shaven, unlike the previous evening, when he had worn a pronounced six o'clock shadow to her house. His hair as usual appeared to be styled by the wind rather than any man-made contrivance.

"And this one you could describe as English country, floral prints and striped wallpaper, in soft, faded colors…"

"Ah! At last I'm getting my striped wallpaper." His mouth curved into that lopsided grin that had a rather unpleasant effect on her stomach.

"No plaid curtains I'm afraid, though."

"What about the horse prints?"

"Not in this room. My plan calls for watercolor paintings of landscapes and flowers, the kind of thing the lady of the house would have painted for her own amusement."

"What if I insist on the horse prints?" He eased his elbows off the desk and settled back into his big leather chair. Something tightened inside Tara at the sight of his broad torso flexing against the hard leather.

"It's your room. You can have it any way you want."

Jesse looked a little disappointed. She certainly wasn't going to let him goad her into any arguments today. "Nah, I like your idea. Paintings by the lady of the house sound nice."

Tara heaved a tiny sigh of relief. But he didn't say another word while she showed him print fabric for the curtains and pictures of period furniture and a fireplace surround.

"Spanish mission style," Jesse murmured, as she revealed a storyboard with pictures of heavy pine furnishings and scrolled ironwork. "I like. My family bought their first acreage from some monks who threw up their hands and headed to Mexico."

"That must have been a long time ago."

"Back before Texas was even a gleam in a politician's eye."

Tara didn't much like the reminder that Jesse was descended from Texas royalty. One more reason for her to feel awkward around him. Especially since her own life was such a shambles.

"Fascinating." She cleared her throat as Jesse reached down to the floor, the soft cotton of his checked shirt straining over his muscled shoulder as he picked up a cat that had wandered in and lifted it onto his lap. He stroked the little ginger kitten under the chin.

"The monks used to ride around on donkeys. My mom always loved donkeys so she convinced my dad to get some as pets. I took my first ride on a donkey."

"You did?" She tried to distract herself from the vision of such a big, powerful man tenderly stroking the tiny kitten.

"Yeah, my mom convinced my dad that a horse would be too much for me. I was only two or three when I started begging to learn. I would have been safer on a horse though, since that donkey had never seen a saddle in her life. She'd buck me off as soon as look at me."

"It's lucky that didn't put you off riding."

"I don't think anything could have put me off riding. I'm not the type that gets put off easily."

The kitten had relaxed back against Jesse, sprawling against his chest with its legs splayed while he rubbed its soft white belly. The sight of those long, powerful fingers moving through the silky fur was doing something entirely disturbing and increasingly uncomfortable in a mysterious spot somewhere down below Tara's belly button.

She shifted in her chair.

"Ahem. The next room is inspired by the Tuscan countryside. Soft, warm colors, aged woods, some antique pottery...."

"What about the horse prints?"

"No prints in this room, only paintings, certainly of the natural world and quite possibly of a horse."

"Well, that's a relief. I thought horses were going to be banned altogether for a minute there." He smiled. An ice-melting, drop-your-stomach-down-to-your-toes, and leave-you-in-a-dripping-heap-on-the-floor smile. Tara forged ahead anyway.

"I know we haven't discussed your budget, and frankly I made my plans on a sort of money-is-no-object basis. I like to start out that way, then figure out where to scale back rather than limiting the project from the outset. Do you have a particular amount that you were planning to spend on the decor?"

"Like I said at the wedding, I was planning to go get some bedspreads and paint. I like your ideas, though, so you go ahead and do it the way you want to and I'll pay whatever it costs." Again he smiled, self-assured, relaxed, good-humored and easy. How infuriating!

"I need a vague idea of what your limits are so I know whether to choose genuine antiques or reproductions, for example."

Whatever he was doing to that cat with his fingers made it loll across him in a furry, purring heap of limp feline ecstasy.

"You're not going to embarrass me by talking about my finances, are you?"

"How do you run a business if you can't talk about money?"

"I don't have any problem talking about money with most people, but with you, I don't know, it just seems...vulgar." One side of his mouth lifted a little more than the other, and he grinned at her lazily. Was he poking fun at her?

"Well, I'm a businesswoman and I'm used to discussing budgets and planning costs."

His eyes were narrowed sleepily, as if he was as relaxed as the cat and about to begin purring, too. Tara felt a warm glow beginning on her cheeks where his eyes rested on them. She had a sudden urge to shock him out of his easy repose.

"How does a hundred thousand dollars sound?" That got his attention. His eyes snapped open, but his hands kept moving lazily over the cat's belly.

"That's a lot of greenbacks for some bedspreads and paint."

"Not really. Fifteen thousand per guest house. It's not even extravagant if you want original paintings and antiques. I'd have to shop around, in fact." She knew she could probably achieve her intended look for less, but she wanted to see Jesse squirm a little. Unfortunately, she was not to have even this slight satisfaction.

"Go for it." He looked at her dead on, good humor still twinkling in his eyes. She had to get away from those eyes, and now.

"Excellent." She gathered her samples back up. He must be even richer than she thought. She was glad for him. Really, she was. He'd obviously worked hard to earn his success and he deserved it. She'd make sure his guesthouses were as beautiful as they could be. That was her profession, and she was good at it.

He placed the cat gently back on the floor and grabbed a stack of fabric samples before she could.

"I think you're the most accommodating client I've ever had," said Tara as he helped her load the samples into the trunk of her suburban.

"I trust your judgment."

"I appreciate that."

It was rather odd having this perfectly ordinary, businesslike exchange with Jesse West. Tara felt a strange little emptiness inside her as she drove away without a single word of innuendo or provocation to rankle over. All business, that was how it was going to be between them from now on. Excellent.

5

Jesse strode out of his barn alongside Bowie and Lucy. He kept looking down the drive to see if Tara was coming. Still no sign of her.

Bowie gestured to an empty pasture to their right. "Now that all the bulls have moved to our place, you've got more room for horses. You should start breeding."

"What makes you think I haven't? I have two mares in foal to my new stallion."

"Bronc prospects?"

"No way." Jesse shook his head. "Fine riding animals. Their mom was a reiner, and their dad a stock horse. I'll see where their talents lie when they make an appearance."

"Very sensible," said Lucy. "I don't know why anyone would breed a horse for broncing when there are so many willing volunteers in people's barns already."

Jesse laughed. "Yep. If they bring 'em to me, I can usually fix 'em. Some, however, are destined for glory in the rodeo ring. No need to breed them for it." He was sure he could hear an engine in the distance.

"Why are you staring down the driveway? Did you ever see that blue truck again?"

"Nope." He wasn't going to tell Bowie that he was lying in wait for Tara. She'd visited his farm twice and manage to slip away without even saying hello to him. He didn't plan to let that happen again, and Manny had informed him that she was coming to meet with a supplier today.

Bowie tried to help Lucy into the truck. "I don't need help," she protested. "Have you forgotten that I exercised three horses this morning?"

"My chivalrous instincts are running out of control."

"Your brother is adorable," she settled herself into the passenger side. "But maddening."

"He's always been that way. Lucky thing he's so lovable. Let me know as soon as you settle on a date for the wedding. I want to book everyone you need before they make other plans."

"You don't think it's obnoxious of us to get married on Valentine's Day?"

"Not at all. It would be awesome. And as I said, we don't have any clients booked yet so we can turn the whole place over to your festivities."

"It's just going to be family and very close friends," explained Lucy. "Bowie's had enough of publicity for one year, and I like things quiet."

"Sounds good to me." Jesse heard an engine and scanned the driveway again. Hay delivery. "I'll make sure the kitchen staff is booked, and you can talk to them about the menu. Is dear old Dad invited?"

"Hell, yes. It's my wedding. He may not be the warmest guy in the world, but he did bring us into it."

Bowie climbed into the driver's seat.

"So you don't believe the rumors that he's the one who tried to frame you for murder?"

"No way. I'm still suspicious of his foreman, but the police couldn't find any hard evidence on him. No one's tried to kill me or frame me for anything in the last month or so, so I'm trying to relax and enjoy life." He squeezed Lucy.

"I still think it had something to do with your land. It's a prime property for mining or ranching."

"I hear ya. My tenant wasn't too happy about leaving."

"I know. He tried to rent from me. I told him I don't have any land to spare."

Bowie looked surprised. "Don't you think that's kind of strange? That he would go from renting one piece of West land to trying to rent another?"

"Not really. I guess he thought he had an 'in' of some kind. It's not easy to rent good ranch land in this area these days. Developers are snapping it up to build new housing. Look at it this way—he'd been renting your land long before you inherited it. Thirty years or more. He'd probably started to believe it was his."

"When did he come here?" Bowie looked around.

"He came about a week and a half ago. No word from him since."

"I'm serious about keeping one eye out for mischief."

"It's hard for anyone to sneak up on me with all my dogs, but I'll keep my eyes peeled."

"I'm not kidding. Whoever tried to set me up for murder did actually kill that woman. I'm not going to stop looking until I find out who it is, either."

"Anything I can do to help, just let me know. So far I haven't seen anything out of the ordinary." Jesse glanced down the driveway again, and his heart lifted to see a big, black Suburban rolling slowly over the gravel. "Tara's here."

Bowie winked at him. "We'd better get going. We'll catch up with you later." Bowie waved to Tara as he passed her in the courtyard at the end of the drive.

Jesse strode toward Tara's car. She'd probably been hoping to sneak in and out without seeing him, because he often gave lessons around this time. Not today.

"Oh, you're here." Tara was startled to see Jesse striding toward her as she emerged from the car. She'd learned from Manny that he was reliably busy at this time of the morning.

"This is my ranch." A slow smile snuck across his mouth, causing turmoil in her insides. "I'd like you to show me what you're working on."

"Of course." She turned from him to get away from his unsettling stare. "Follow me."

She led him into the cottage that was farthest along, and he stomped up the stairs to the bedroom, big boots making too much noise on the bare wood stairs. His dark eyes appraised the woodwork, before assaulting hers with that steady gaze that made her breathing turn shallow. "That looks like it came from an old barn."

"Doesn't it? The painter uses milk paint, then wipes some off the edges with a damp cloth before it dries. I think she did an amazing job." There, see? She managed to sound quite calm. Businesslike, even. She could do this.

They were in the French country cottage, and the soft pale blue of the milk paint—from her stockpile of her own branded line—contrasted beautifully with the gray-brown stained wood.

"Looks good, all the rooms do."

"Thanks." She smiled and wished this wasn't so awkward. Larger than life, smelling deliciously of horses and the outdoors, Jesse disturbed the quiet air of the room like a cyclone. She'd rather deal with snooty investment bankers any day. They were far more predictable.

"You're wearing jeans."

"Yes," Tara drifted a little further off kilter. "Is there a dress code for the job that I'm not aware of?"

"If there was one, jeans would be right at the top of the list." He smiled. "I was thinking, since you're dressed for it, maybe you'd like to go for a little ride with me."

"On a horse?"

"Well, yeah, I'm fresh out of donkeys right now and the bulls have just moved to Bowie's place. Can you ride?"

"Sure." She'd been on a pony ride on the beach once or twice, nothing to it. She didn't want him to think she was a total loser.

"Can you get away right now? I've got a couple of appointments lined up later, but the next two hours are all mine."

"Er, I don't think so." Spending too much time with Jesse had a dangerous effect on her. And the trim carpenter was going to be there in half an hour and she had some pictures to show him. "I've got some appointments lined up myself."

"I'm sure Manny can take care of them. He's way into the whole project, fancies himself as a regular decorator these days. Hey, Manny!"

Unfortunately, Manny was within earshot and more than willing to pick up the slack.

"It'll be fun. You'll get to see some of the country around here. And I've got just the right horse for you. She reminds me a little of you, in fact."

"Blond mane?"

"Nah, she's spotted."

"Oh, thanks."

"Spots are a good thing on a horse. Appaloosa, very smart, nice mover. It's her personality that reminds me of you. Most of the time she's cool as a cucumber but every now and then some kind of fire will light up inside her and she'll buck and head for the hills." She saw a quick flash of his crooked grin before he turned from her to open the pasture gate.

This was Jesse's first reference to her energetic departure, which naturally implied a reference to the events that had preceded it. She didn't know whether to be more nervous about the fact that he was bringing up what happened between them, or the suggestion that he was putting her on a potential runaway horse.

"That doesn't sound too safe."

"Don't you worry. I've been working with her for months. She's gentle as a lamb. She just needs to know that you're the boss, and I have the idea you don't have a problem letting anyone know you're in charge."

Tara watched Jesse tack up her mount himself while one of his assistants got his horse ready. The brown-and-white-spotted mare did appear friendly as

Tara gingerly patted her neck.

Jesse seemed sweetly excited at the prospect of going for a ride with her. He was very solicitous, finding her a helmet that fit just right, adjusting her stirrups, telling her how great she looked on the horse.

Tara's heart was pounding as he mounted his own horse and they set off on a trail into the woods. The trail was wide enough for them to ride side by side. Tara watched and imitated how he held the reins and sat up straight in the saddle, and she thought she was doing a creditable job of looking like she could actually ride.

Since she'd had to sneak a few peeks at him to perfect her technique, she had unfortunately noticed how comfortably his firm backside settled in the saddle. And his thighs were powerful. All muscle.

"How long have you owned this place?"

"Seven years now. I inherited it when my mom died. She'd had my dad parcel off pieces of the ranch so she could leave some land to each of us, just to have as our own."

"It's beautiful."

"Sure is. I've been wanting to move here since the moment I saw it. Just had to finish running around riding bulls for good, and here I am."

Did it get any better than this? Jesse didn't think so. It was a beautiful sunny day. He was out riding—his favorite thing to do—and sitting on the horse next to him was the girl of his dreams.

He sneaked a quick look at her. Perfect. The morning sun illuminated her delicate features and lit up her soft pale hair where it was escaping from the helmet. He'd been careful to choose a quiet horse for her since she probably hadn't ridden in a few years. He'd told her that story about the horse running off just to see those blue eyes widen a little, but he'd never put her on a spooky horse.

The way her lovely behind rested in that saddle he could see that she was a natural. He wouldn't mind being that saddle for an hour or two. He'd been very good about keeping his distance from her as she came and went from the ranch over the past couple of weeks, supervising the work, but if he kept his distance from her too well, the job would be over and she'd be gone and that would be the end of that.

He let his eyes rest on her for a moment. She looked relaxed, cheerful, and she seemed to be enjoying her ride. "How do you like ChaCha?"

"ChaCha?"

"Yeah, short for ChaChaCha. She does it in the paddock sometimes when she thinks no one's looking." There, he got a smile. Ah, that made him feel good.

"She's nice. I like the polka dots."

"I told you spots would suit you. Want to go a little faster?"

"Sure."

So far so good. This riding thing was a piece of cake. She could see why people liked it. It was a nice, relaxing way to get out into the countryside. His horse started trotting, at least that was what she thought it was called. Hers didn't seem to be doing much of anything, so she kicked it with her legs a little.

Woah! The horse lurched forward, and she grabbed at the mane as it popped up and down like a pogo stick. One hand came loose from the mane and flailed in the air as she dropped the reins. She bounced wildly in the saddle, her stirrups long gone, one hand clutching a fistful of mane and the other clinging desperately to the saddle.

"Shall we canter?" His voice penetrated her terror-numbed ears.

"No!" The panic in her voice made him turn his head and quickly wheel his horse around and grab her reins.

The initial look of shock and concern on his face creased into a broad grin after he had their horses halted.

"You said you could ride."

"I guess I lied." She could feel her face blazing. Her terror had turned into a sudden hot flash of embarrassment mingled with anger for letting herself get lured into this predicament. She kept trying to get her feet back into the stirrups, but she couldn't seem to find them. "We didn't all spend our childhoods on a ranch, you know."

"I know, I just figured you'd taken lessons somewhere along the way. Most girls do, don't they?"

"Somehow I never did." Most of the girls at the exclusive Andover Academy, which she'd attended with Jesse, probably did, but her parents' income swung wildly—along with her father's gambling success—so she'd never had the luxury. And she still couldn't get a foot in either one of those damn stirrups.

"I guess I've gotten used to being surrounded by girls whose daddy bought them a pony for Christmas." He cocked his head to the side, looking for her reaction.

"Well, lucky them." She tried to act nonchalant, but she felt a surge of irritation at the thought of all those girls with their damned ponies draping themselves over Jesse. What did she care? They were welcome to him.

"How are you supposed to get your feet back into these things anyway?"

"Here." He'd maneuvered his horse up next to hers and he leaned over and twisted her stirrup leather around as she slipped her foot in. "Hold on, I'll get the other side for you too." He dismounted and helped her get her foot back in.

He put his hand on her thigh. Reassuringly. At least that's what she assumed it was supposed to be.

"Are you okay, princess?"

"Tara. And, yes, of course I'm okay."

His hand patted her thigh. "We'll walk from now on."

"Good." He lifted his hand off her thigh, but the skin underneath her jeans burned hotly as if he'd left a brand there.

He climbed back on his horse. "You did great, hanging in there."

"I dropped the reins! There's no need to patronize me, I'm not an idiot."

They were walking along the trail side by side. Tara would have loved to turn back to the barn, but she wasn't willing to look like a quitter.

"You didn't fall off."

"Another couple of seconds and I might well have."

"You have a very natural seat and leg position. I had no idea you couldn't ride. You should learn."

"I don't think so. I've never been too interested in

horses."

She immediately regretted her dismissive comment. Sometimes she could be so arrogant she disgusted herself. All he wanted was to be friendly and share his love of horses with her. It wasn't his fault she was too pretentious to let him know she'd never taken a riding lesson in her life. Perfect Tara, she just hated to have anyone find out that there was something she couldn't do.

"Horses can be a little intimidating if you're not used to them, but once you get hooked there's no turning back."

"Well, I'm just trying to recover from getting hooked on cigarettes so I'm going to be a little more cautious about diving into addictive activities in the future."

"I can't picture you smoking." He looked really surprised. She was surprised she'd told him. Hardy anyone knew she smoked as she had rarely done it in public. Only when she was with Gordon or alone. She'd been good at concealing her secret vice.

"Hopefully it's a picture no one will ever see again. I haven't had one in a few weeks now."

"Good. Those things will kill you, you know."

"I'd heard."

"Seriously, though, I'd be happy to give you some riding lessons. It's one of those skills you should have, like learning how to swim or drive a car."

"Oddly enough my life experience has never called for expert horsemanship. But you never know. I might get caught in a shoot-out while decorating a Western saloon and have to make a break for it on a half-wild mustang."

Jesse nodded soberly. "It could happen."

"Riding looks so easy!"

"It is easy, once you get the hang of it." He smiled at her. "I'm telling you, you're a natural. Most people take weeks of lessons to learn to keep their legs in the right place. It'll be fun to teach you to ride. Don't worry, we'll make up for your deprived childhood."

"It was hardly deprived. Besides, we did have horses in the family. My dad was always buying shares in racehorses and losing tons of money on them."

Jesse chuckled. "Maybe you should buy a horse. This time get the whole thing."

She lifted a brow. "I don't think the zoning in my neighborhood would allow that."

"Why do you live in that neighborhood? It doesn't seem like your style."

A wave of indignation swept through her. "Why not?"

"You own a seven-bedroom house with a three-car garage." His eyes danced with suppressed laughter. At least he was suppressing it. She didn't want to be openly laughed at right now, much as she deserved it. "And there's only one of you."

"There were two of us, you'll recall." She and Gordon had chosen it together. "And it only has six bedrooms. It was a good investment. We were planning for the future when we bought it." Though it was in both their names, Gordon had paid for it. After he left, she studied the paperwork and realized he'd somehow put no money down at all and the mortgage debt had actually grown, so that when he signed the house over to her, he was actually sinking her deeper into debt.

Jesse turned toward her, one hand holding his reins loosely and the other resting on his thigh. "You were planning for the six kids to ride in your big Suburban"

"I guess so, yeah." She looked at him and shrugged. "Pathetic, isn't it?"

"I don't think so. I think it's kind of sweet." His smile seemed genuine. Ugh, he had to be a nice guy still. That was annoying. She preferred it when he was ticking her off, at least then she didn't feel so bad about the way she'd dumped him to run back to Gordon.

"I always was a planner."

"And I wasn't part of your plan."

"Nope, you weren't part of the plan." She turned to look at him deliberately, to see what his reaction would be. She'd expected to see yet another phase of that sneaky grin that seemed to play across his face so often when he looked at her. She was surprised to see no humor there at all. He looked pensive, as if he had a question on his lips for a second, then thought better of it. They rode in silence for a while.

"You're trying to sell it."

"Your observational skills are impressive. As you said, it's too much for me." Taking the job at Jesse's would let her stay afloat for at least a couple more months. Hopefully it would sell by then.

"So you do deviate from your plans?" he asked, tilting his head slightly as he looked at her.

"Not often." *Though sometimes they deviate from me.* "I'm usually pretty thorough about thinking things through and coming up with the right game plan from the start. That's important in my business. If you start making last-minute changes and additions you won't come in on time and on budget. I work my butt off to make sure everything goes according to plan."

"From what I can see it looks like there's just enough of it left to sit on." He let his eyes wander deliberately to her backside, as it swayed and rolled with the movement of the horse's back. Tara felt a little surge of heat rising from the part of her that was touching the saddle.

She knew his eyes were resting on her, and she became very conscious of the way her legs lay curved around the broad body of the horse. Her thighs probably looked really fat from his angle, but Jesse's face registered nothing but approval.

His warm, appreciative gaze, and all that shifting and moving of the horse under her shook up some rather provoking sensations inside her. She could feel her nipples firming up beneath her blouse, and she let herself enjoy the little tingle of pleasure that zipped down to her belly button.

She looked at Jesse and smiled. He was a sexy guy, and he knew it. Easy animal grace packed into a powerful frame. His dark brown eyes met hers with a little electric jolt that ricocheted between them. Ouch, her crotch heated up against the saddle in a way that was a little too arousing. It was time to try to get some of this pulsing blood circulating back up to her brain again.

"You're lucky that you found something you love to do. A lot of people live their whole lives without reaching that point."

"What about you? Is interior design what you love to do?" The way he wrapped his tongue carefully around the words *interior design*. It certainly didn't sound like something that could be anyone's passion.

"I do enjoy it. It gives me independence, control

over my own schedule, the satisfaction of a job well done. I like being in business for myself." *At least when there's money coming in.*

"Are you happy?" He asked it earnestly, his face serious.

"The million-dollar question." She smiled. Of course she was happy. Everyone knew that. She'd always been happy. It's easy to be happy when you're perfect. And wasn't she perfect Princess Tara?

He was watching her, waiting for an answer.

Saying yes would be easy enough. But she didn't want to. Maybe it was time to stop putting on a show for everyone and for herself. She didn't even know what happy was. She probably never had—that was why all her careful planning and exacting execution had made her exactly who she was right now: pretty, perfect Tara with her big, empty house and her big, empty life.

Faking it was easy. Having it was a whole different story.

"Maybe being happy doesn't come naturally to me. I don't think I've ever been really happy. I'm always waiting for something amazing to happen, but strangely it never does."

"Sounds like it's time for you to stop waiting and start working on plan B." He smiled.

"I suppose I should. The failure of plan A is all a little bit fresh and raw still."

"I had a feeling it was."

"You're not going to make me cry again, are you?" She suddenly felt very small and vulnerable. God knows he probably could make her cry at the blink of an eye, let alone the touch of those strange magic hands. She was that close to the edge a lot of the time these days.

"Not unless you want me to. I'd rather see you smile."

"I'd rather see me smile, too."

Back at the barn Jesse dismounted and came around the side of her horse to help her down. He stood behind her as she swung her leg over, and he put his hands on her hips, easing her down to the ground. Her backside brushed against him as she came down, sparking an awkward frisson of pleasure.

Letting her blood sizzle a little while they sat a horse's length apart was very different from having it approach boiling point when there were no barriers between them, as she knew from the experience in the guest bedroom. She stepped away from him quickly.

"I'm sure I'll be walking bowlegged for days."

"Did you enjoy the ride?"

"I did. I enjoyed the ride and the company." The truth. It felt odd being honest, but maybe it was a good experiment to work on for a while. "Except for the part where I made a complete ass out of myself and probably scared the daylights out of the horse by flopping around like a sack of potatoes and dropping the reins."

"That won't happen again. Next time you'll know what to expect. Will there be a next time? Will you let me give you a lesson in the arena?" He looked so eager that she couldn't bring herself to say no.

"Maybe. We'll see how much pain I'm in tomorrow morning."

"You'll be fine. You're in great shape, as I couldn't help noticing." He had a flirty twinkle in his eye that made her feel a bit reckless.

"You're not in such rough shape yourself." He laughed and looked a little embarrassed. Men probably didn't get too many personal compliments. "Though you probably don't have to use a Stairmaster to stay that way."

"Nope, the stairs up to the hayloft do the trick for me."

They hesitated, not sure how to take leave of each other. They'd obviously taken a step beyond the purely business relationship they'd cultivated over the past couple of weeks, and neither of them wanted to step too far and fall off the precipice again, either.

Tara could only stand but so much of a pregnant pause before her need to organize, to tidy up loose ends, got the better of her. "I've got some phone calls to make. I'm going to L.A. next week, but I'll stop by when I get back, to see how things are coming along."

6

Tara drove up Jesse's long driveway with a tingle of nervous excitement pricking at her fingertips and making her breathe a little faster. It had been relatively easy putting him out of her mind while she was in L.A. since she was immersed in a different world. She'd gone there to discuss set design for a new show and wound up having several conversations about possibly hosting her own show on HGTV. Apparently, word of her paint line going under had not reached the West Coast. Maybe she could even turn the whole thing around if she had a platform like that. She called the paint manufacturer she owed money to and they agreed to hold off on demanding their debt until the end of the month.

But now she was back, Jesse kept sneaking into her thoughts at the most inopportune moments.

She parked and surreptitiously scanned the area for him. Part of her wanted to run into a guesthouse, examine the trim carpenter's work and scurry back to her car without coming across him. Some other part of her craved the sight of his warm smile and the rush of being appraised by those bold, dark eyes.

No sign of him so far. She crossed the gravel courtyard and walked along the stone path to the cottages, where she examined the carpentry and found it wonderfully well done. She was heading back to her car with a mild sense of disappointment at having successfully avoided her client when Manny approached her and told her that Jesse was in the arena shooting a video and wanted to see her before she left.

Manny led her over to the fenced sand arena, surrounded by a strip of manicured grass. Jesse stood on the far side talking to a tall woman in jeans and a red shirt. Tara watched from the edge, not wanting to interrupt their conversation as the woman brushed a hand over the front of Jesse's shirt.

He laughed, then the woman chimed in, and Tara suffered an odd twinge of annoyance. She was doing something with the front of his shirt, straightening the buttons, maybe? Then she bent down and started brushing at his jeans, still talking and smiling. Jesse was looking rather cheerful, too.

Hmph. Looks like I'm interrupting something, thought Tara. She turned to tell Manny that she'd give Jesse a call that afternoon, but Manny had already vanished. She cleared her throat. Jesse's head snapped around and his face creased into a grin.

"Hi, Tara." He strode toward her. "Thanks for dropping in."

"What was that girl doing to you?" Her voice came out far more high-pitched than she had intended, accusatory, even, and she immediately felt embarrassed.

"Primping me. I guess I always have a layer of dust on me that needs to be brushed off." He smiled. "We're shooting a video about communicating with your horse. There's one more scene to shoot, and then they're packing up for the day. I was hoping you'd have lunch with me."

Panic flashed through her. "Oh, I really can't. I have to draw some sketches for a client I'm seeing tomorrow."

But those could wait until later if you want to insist.

"Please have lunch with me. I've got roast chicken and a big salad back at my house. We can eat outside since it's such a beautiful day." He glanced over to the woman, who was talking to the cameraman, then looked back at Tara, his face earnest. "I'll tell them we'll have to shoot this scene another time."

Now that was the type of cajoling, begging even, that she needed. And it *was* unseasonably warm and beautiful. Why waste such a lovely day? It was in the mid seventies, despite being December.

"Okay, I'll have lunch with you. But shoot the scene first. I'll watch."

Now that he'd wooed her so energetically she didn't feel jealous when he walked back over to the other woman. Not even when that woman had her hands practically in his underpants as she fiddled around attaching the microphone to the back of his jeans.

Tara watched as Jesse mounted his horse and circled around the arena, talking about some horsey concept she didn't understand while he rode. He was smiling. Smiling probably a little bit too much to be appropriate for a horse video, and she knew that she had put that smile on his face.

People would be sitting in their living rooms, trying to pick up tips about horsemanship and wondering why Jesse West had a big goofy grin on his face. It made her chuckle, and it made her feel good.

Jesse led her along the broad stone path to his house. It was the first time she'd been inside it.

"I just have to grab our lunch, then we can go sit by the pond." He opened the door and let her inside. Several dogs instantly accosted them, and one jumped up at her, nails threatening to catch on the fabric of her pale linen suit.

"Down, Junior!" The black-and-white mutt backed off apologetically.

"Goodness, you have a lot of dogs." Fondled by their master, the motley crew wandered back to their business.

"Only four."

"That's a lot." She couldn't imagine the havoc that four dogs might wreak inside a house, but obviously Jesse took it in stride.

His house was very clearly a man's home. She couldn't see a single feminine touch anywhere. No pictures on the walls, no knickknacks, just simple, heavy furniture in neutral colors and practical functional objects. There was an old saddle upturned against one wall, but otherwise the space was neat and clean.

His house had good bones. If it were hers she'd paint the maple kitchen cabinets cream and replace the beige counter with a slab of soapstone. And wide pine floorboards would look better than the oak strips.

Tara! Cease and desist! Redecorating the world around her was a hard habit to break.

"Maybe I should have asked the architect for six bedrooms. Right now there are four. It's just the right size for one man and a few dogs and cats."

Tara began to notice the cats. She could see three of them from where she was standing, and another came into view, sidling out from behind the enormous vintage fridge as Jesse opened the door and started rooting around inside it.

Two of the dogs had curled up on the sofa, but a chastened Junior walked hesitantly back to Tara and stood at her feet looking up at her with cautious blue eyes. She bent down and ruffled the fur at his neck.

"How come you have so many pets?"

"They turned up, one by one."

"Strays?"

"Yup." He turned to look at her and smiled to see her rubbing Junior's belly as he rolled enthusiastically on the floor under her moving hand. "Junior there showed up one night injured and bleeding. I think he got into a fight with a coyote. I patched him up and he stuck around. Similar deal with the other dogs. The cats come and go as they please."

"Don't the cats fight with the dogs?"

"Sure." He smiled. "Can't expect everyone to get along all the time."

Jesse was so laid-back and easygoing. If she was going to get a pet, she would research it for months, weighing the pros and cons of choosing one particular breed over another, then looking into the most reputable breeders and which was their absolutely most promising stock.

Not a wonder she'd never owned a pet, really. Even one animal might be an intrusive disruption of her serene home environment, yet Jesse accepted an entire menagerie with its attendant spats and discord as a normal part of life. She and Jesse were about as different as two people could get.

"I think I've got everything. Do you like iced tea?"

"I love it. What can I carry?"

"You could grab that blanket off the couch. We can use it as a picnic blanket."

"Okay." She folded it up under her arm and followed Jesse back out in the blinding midday sunlight. She saw a pair of bluebirds chasing each other through the branches of a sapling, and fat squirrels playing hide-and-seek on the trunk of an oak tree.

"It's so quiet here, aren't there any roads nearby?"

"I'm down in a valley, so you can't hear any traffic. Do you like my place?"

"I love it. It's heavenly. I thought I had a big property with my measly quarter-acre."

"It all depends what you're used to. Since I grew up on a big ranch, any place where you can see another house feels like the big city to me. I prefer a little peace and privacy." They came out of the woods into a clearing filled with a glittering lake. An area to one side of the lake had been planted with grass and there was a small dock there.

"My fishing hole."

"Do you fish?"

"No, never. But I like the idea that I could." He chuckled. "Let's spread out the blanket on the grass over there."

Jesse lay on his side, eased along one edge of the blanket. Tara sat cross-legged on the other side, nibbling at her salad. He took bites of chicken, washed down with iced tea, all the time watching Tara, his dark eyes shining with amusement.

"Do you do everything neatly?"

"I try to."

"Don't you ever get tired of being perfect?"

"I'm not even close to being perfect."

"Yes, you are. More than you know." He grinned lazily at her, and she felt a little flame flicker alight somewhere down inside her. "It must be a heavy burden needing to do everything right all the time."

"It would be better if I tried to do stuff wrong?"

He shook his head, smiling. "Nope, but sometimes you've gotta just do stuff, and figure out the right or wrong part later."

"That kind of behavior sounds like it could get you into trouble."

"Yeah," his smile broadened into a grin. His eyes narrowed slightly and flashed as the sunlight caught them. "That's exactly what I'm talking about."

She told him about the TV show opportunity that had come out of nowhere and might still amount to nothing. He was impressed, which cheered her. Eventually, he wiped his fingers on a napkin and sat up, shifting closer to her on the blanket. He rested his elbows on his knees and looked at her. She noticed a crumb on his white shirt, and she reached forward instinctively to brush it off.

"Primping me?"

"Yes. You need it."

"Do I? I guess I don't care too much about not looking perfect."

"You don't have to. You've got something that a lot of people would kill for, natural style, effortless elegance. And I say that based on my professional experience."

"Really?" He raised his eyebrows and contemplated what she said, a smile playing across his lips. "I like that. It means a lot, coming from you."

"Coming from Tara Kent, style maven, or Princess Tara from Andover Academy?"

He looked at her for an agonizingly long moment, amusement still curving the corners of his mouth. "They're one and the same, aren't they?"

"You tell me." She felt almost as if someone else was talking through her. Jesse's presence in front of her, big and close, was making her feel reckless and a little crazy.

Jesse rose up on to his knees, a strange look in his dark eyes. "I might need to—" but she never knew what he might need to do because at that moment his lips settled over hers and a hot blast of sensation made her thoughts flutter away like dried leaves.

She leaned into him as they wrapped eager arms around each other. She held him close, inhaling his raw, male scent and losing her fingers in his hair. Jesse's mouth made a trail of kisses to her ear, where he breathed hotly, triggering a tremor that shook her to her toes and made her gasp with longing.

Together they eased down onto the blanket, until she lay sprawled under him. His warm tongue penetrated the soft wetness of her mouth, teasing and taunting her with flickering movements.

His long fingers roamed her clothes, caressed the arching hollow of her back, gently squeezed her backside and thighs. As his fingers moved carefully over her hips to lightly cover the zipper of her pants, she moaned, desire burning between her legs.

She clutched at his shirt as he pushed his hard belly to hers, stoking the fire as still-clothed flesh itched to touch flesh. Her teeth grazed his hard cheekbone. She wanted him, her body pounding with alien need. Desperate and hungry, she pushed him, shoving him with arms and elbows, rolling on top of him and taking control.

She rubbed her breasts against him, and his hands rose to greet them, kneading and thumbing her nipples until she was gasping for breath. Her pelvis pushed against his, and she felt the hard arrow of his arousal behind the zipper of his jeans.

"Jesse," she whispered. Her eyes opened and met his, which were black with urgent longing. In a flash they had rolled again and he was back on top of her. His agile tongue flickered torment over the throbbing pulse points behind her ears. Her body shuddered as he sucked hard on a tender earlobe.

His hands roved inside her bra, stroking her painfully excited nipples so gently that she wanted to scream, his feather touch building her excitement to an unbearable fever pitch.

Then he stopped.

His face creased into an expression of agony. "I don't have a condom. I wasn't expecting—"

"I'm on the Pill, I'm protected," she rasped hoarsely. "Please."

She wanted him so badly that it hurt.

"Please…"

Her eyes were closed tight, her hands gripping at his neck as he shoved off his jeans, pushed down her pants and panties and gently guided himself inside her.

Oh.

It felt so good.

Jesse.

For a moment they stayed completely still, him inside her, where he was meant to be.

She felt his maleness dancing in response to the

intimate caress of her soft insides even as the rest of their bodies remained motionless. His cheek pressed against hers and she held him, glorying in the perfect intimacy of the moment.

She felt whole, warm, needed and loved.

And then he started to move.

His hips rocked as he moved over her, moaning softly. Her hips arched up to his as every nerve in her body hummed.

Each hot note singing in her blood seemed to drive her further into herself, closer to Jesse, as their souls reached out through the tormented flesh of their bodies.

She wanted to stay like this for all eternity.

No, she wanted more, she wanted to go deeper, pull herself closer to Jesse until there were no more barriers between them.

As his body pushed into hers and hers opened to welcome it, the howling of her blood in her ears, the singing in her veins and the thrumming of her nerves grew louder, deafening, as she felt herself moving in slow, pulsing motion toward the edge of a glistening precipice.

This is it.

Which of them had said it? Had it been said or only thought?

She couldn't hear, she couldn't think, images and sensations crowded her, drawing her deeper into a magical netherworld where nothing existed but her and Jesse, drawing deeper, closer, fusing together and becoming one throbbing, humming, singing, pulsating being.

You're the one.

As the words echoed through her body she felt

herself crashing hard over the edge of that precipice, splashing down into the dark water below and drifting away on rhythmic tides that swept her far, far out to sea, into the shoreless blackness of a moonless night.

When she opened her eyes, Jesse was leaning over her. Unconcealed relief lit up his face.

"What happened?" Her voice didn't sound like hers any more. She felt disoriented, disembodied.

"You lost consciousness, passed out. Scared the hell out of me." He reached out his hand and softly pushed a strand of hair out of her eyes.

Tara tested her body to see if she could move. All systems seemed to be in good working order. She felt a little woozy as she tried to lift her head, and she lay it back down in the soft grass. Jesse leaned forward and kissed her softly on the cheek.

"I don't know what came over me." She was oddly relaxed for someone recovering from an unexpected fainting episode. The sunlight warmed her, and Jesse's solicitous presence made her feel safe.

"I think I do." He picked up one of her hands and stroked it softly. He turned her hand gently over and ran a finger along the length of her lifeline, then looked up into her eyes.

"I read once about something called *le petit mort*. That's French for 'the little death.' It's a loss of consciousness that happens to some people when they have an orgasm. It's rare. Has it ever happened to you before?"

"No. But then I've never..." She looked at him.

I've never felt anything like that before.

She'd never had an orgasm like that with Gordon. She and her ex had sex, but she could see now that they had never truly made love. That was what she and Jesse had done—they had made love. And there it was, shining between them in the sunlight.

Jesse eased himself down into the grass and nestled up close to her. They'd somehow rolled a few feet away from the blanket, but the warm, soft grass was more comfortable than any fabric under their skin.

He wrapped his arm around her and kissed her gently.

"Are you okay, Tara?"

"I don't know. I don't know what I am."

"That's all right." He said softly. "I'll take care of you."

And at that moment, that was enough.

He held her and they basked in the warmth of the sun. Then Jesse looked at her and a mischievous grin crept across his face.

"I've had a glimpse of the raging inferno under that cool-as-a-cucumber exterior of yours. What I want to know is if that fire is burning away there all the time or does it only flare right up when I'm around?"

She blinked. She could swear she'd never even made a noise during sex in her whole life. She'd sort of lost control, though, when Jesse was doing...whatever it was he was doing.

"Don't blush! I like your wild side. I like all your sides and everything inside as well." He smiled and touched her chin gently with his thumb.

"You have grass in your hair," she said.

"So do you." He gently plucked a strand of grass out of her tousled mane. "It suits you. You should wear it more often."

His big, satisfied grin gave Tara an odd tickle of pleasure and an equal and opposite prickle of indignation.

"You look like the Cheshire cat, grinning from ear to ear like that, or the cat that swallowed the canary, or some other clichéd metaphor about fat, happy cats."

"How about a lion, the big old king of the jungle, happy to be spending some idle time with his queen?"

"We are being pretty idle, aren't we?"

"Nothing wrong with that, if the time is right. I could get used to being idle with you." His smile softened into a more cautious expression. He paused and touched her hand. "I could get used to being with you."

Uh-oh. He'd done it. He'd gone too far, he could see it in her face. He'd gotten a little carried away there, thinking of himself as the king of the jungle with his queen. And she was a queen all right, her hair a golden crown, her eyes perfect blue sapphires, her skin glowing like honey in the warm afternoon sun.

Their sex had been more intense than ever—an act of Love, with a capital L, on his part at least. And she'd been right there with him; he knew she had, he could feel it.

That had given him a scare when she blacked out like that. For a second he'd wondered if he should give her the kiss of life or call for help. But then he'd remembered. *Le petit mort.*

Not the kind of thing you expect to run across in the day-to-day course of events, but then Tara was no ordinary woman, never had been. Now he knew one more of her magical secrets.

Looking at her lying there in the grass, he could see her getting a little restless, pondering what to do next. Going with the flow did not come naturally to Tara. But there was no denying that she'd flowed far down the river with him today. Any further and they both would have needed a life raft to come back.

"Let me fix your clothes."

She nodded, still languid with spent passion. He pulled her panties back up, soft creamy satin with lace, delicate in his big, clumsy-looking fingertips. He eased up her jeans, raising them slowly, savoring the honeyed fullness of her thighs, tucking her soft shirt in neatly before fastening the buttons and re-zipping the zipper.

"You're good to go." He sneaked a soft kiss on her lips.

"Thanks." She smiled, still basking a little in the afterglow of their lovemaking. God she was beautiful, more beautiful than he'd ever seen her.

He pulled his own jeans back on and crawled around in the grass hunting for the boots he'd kicked off so hastily. He didn't want their interlude to end, but he also wanted to end on a high note. This was a tentative first step in their very fragile new relationship. He didn't want to push his luck and frighten her back into her shell.

This time was going to be different. He wouldn't let her push him away. He wasn't going to push himself on her, either. Jesse West was going to follow his own advice on how to gentle a wild-eyed horse: He was going to take it slow, get it right and make it last.

7

"Darling, you know enough about me to lead to my arrest and conviction for any number of crimes at a moment's notice. Your secrets are safe with me. You can tell me anything, you know that." She heard Melody pull hard on one of her extra long Sobranies.

Tara's hair was still wet from the shower and her hands shook a little, nicotine withdrawal probably. She'd floated home from Jesse's on a cloud, but now that she was away from him the cloud had evaporated and she felt very alone and not a little frightened by what had happened between them.

"Well, we, uh, we made love."

"Good for you!"

"Outside on the grass."

"All right! I bet you never screwed out under the sun with Gordon."

"Good lord, no." You never had to worry about doing anything crazy with Gordon. That had been one of the things, most of them now rather hard to recall, that she had liked about him. "And something weird happened."

"What? Go on!"

"I fainted."

"You swooned? Passed out?"

"Yes. It happened when I, er, when I had an—" How could she put it delicately?

"Orgasm."

"Yes." It was a relief that at least one of them could come right out and say things.

"I bet you never had an orgasm with Gordon, did you?"

"I thought I had, but I guess not."

"Welcome to the world of the sexually satisfied woman. I'm raising my glass to you. And Jesse West has just shot up immeasurably on my 'Is he the one for Tara?' counter."

"But I blacked out! That's hardly a good thing."

"I read about that in *Cosmo* once." Tara heard Melody take another drag of her cigarette. "I always hoped I'd be dramatic enough to experience it, but no. You, however, are apparently made of more erotically ecstatic stuff than I."

Tara ran a hand over her face. Everyone seemed to have heard of this crazy thing except her. She hadn't wasted her teenage years reading magazines, though, or having sex.

"But what if I pass out and don't wake up again?"

"At least you'd die happy, darling."

"Melody! Be serious. I don't think I ever want to experience that again."

"Then you need to find someone else like Gordon so there won't be any danger of you experiencing sexual ecstasy again. And, no, I'm *not* recommending that course of action."

Tara didn't like her feelings for Jesse. They weren't predictable or controllable. They weren't safe.

While they were going at it like rabbits under the

sun, she'd actually become delusional enough to feel like she was in love.

And this only weeks after being dumped by the man she'd planned to spend the rest of her life with.

Clearly she was experiencing some kind of rebound madness.

It didn't help that it was Christmastime, and for the first time in years she didn't have a partner to share it with. Maybe that's why she'd run headlong into an old flame's arms. She and Jesse couldn't be more different. It couldn't possibly ever work out. If he had any sense he'd fall in love with someone free-spirited and untamed like him—maybe even a horse trainer like Bowie's fiancée—and she'd go sloping off alone.

Pursuing a relationship with him was a road to nowhere, and she was just setting herself up for more heartbreak every time she let his slow smile cross her mind.

Weighed down with debts and on the brink of losing her home, she needed to keep her mind off this distracting cowboy and focused on her career and selling this damn house.

Speaking of which, she decided to refinish the fireplace. The elaborate seasonal display of antique silver and mercury glass votives that she'd carefully assembled, looked garish against the white mantel. She decided to strip it back to the natural wood and refinish it darker, so she was high on paint-stripper fumes when the doorbell rang.

Maybe she shouldn't answer it. Those Jehovah's Witnesses had already stopped by three times this year. Apparently, someone had noted in their records that she was in urgent need of spiritual salvation.

Then again, maybe it was the UPS man and she was waiting for a delivery of some samples she wanted to take to L.A. with her. She climbed up off her knees and headed for the door.

"Hi, Tara." It was Jesse, larger than life—as usual—bearing a big bunch of pink roses. "Can I come in?"

Pink roses? Uh-oh. Her heart squeezed. What was he trying to do to her?

She opened the door and let him into the foyer. The rug had dried out, but there was a big ripple in the middle of it where the fibers of the backing had buckled. She was hoping it would settle down of its own accord; if not it was going to cost a fortune to get it fixed. She stared at it, avoiding that disturbing gaze of his.

"It reeks in here!"

"I'm stripping something."

"That sounds sexy."

"Not really." She pointed to the fireplace, which looked naked and ashamed with its finish all buckled and half scraped off. She felt a bit like that herself after what happened last time they were together. "What are you doing here?"

"I came to give you these," he indicated the bunch of roses. There must have been thirty or more of them. "Did you think I was carrying them around in case they came in handy?"

"They're lovely." She took them from him and lifted the bouquet to her nose. The scent of roses was her favorite smell in the world. If only they weren't from the one man that seemed to turn her into a madwoman. "I'll put them in some water."

She got out a cut-glass vase for the roses and

began to snip off the ends of the stems and arrange them. Jesse followed her into the kitchen and watched her silently. His steady gaze increasingly unnerved her until her hands started shaking. "What are you looking at?"

"You." His face was covered with a big smile.

"Is something funny?"

"No, just nice."

"Why? You like seeing me when I'm wearing baggy shorts and an old T-shirt?"

"Yes."

He continued to watch her in silence. Apparently, he didn't feel the need to talk. The quiet, punctuated only by the snipping of her scissors and the occasional drip of water, was making Tara nervous.

He probably did enjoy watching her wearing her most hideously unflattering working-with-paint clothes. That would be just like him to want to see her when she wasn't looking her best. Maybe it was part of his ongoing strategy to peel away her thin veneer of respectability that kept the outside world from seeing what a mess she really was.

She snipped at the stems, feeling her temperature rise. "Did you ever hear of calling before you come over?"

"I'm not too crazy about phones. Things don't always come out right when you're talking through technology. I wanted to see your face."

"Well, here it is. Totally devoid of makeup, I hope you like it."

There she went, getting all hot under the collar again. That was the last thing he wanted. He wondered why she got mad so easily when he was around. He didn't think flying into a rage was her usual MO. He strongly suspected it was because she liked him. And she didn't like that.

He did like seeing her face without makeup. He did like seeing her not dressed up. Looking the way she would if they were at home together.

Why couldn't she see that they were meant for each other? Opposites, sure, there was no doubt that they were opposites, but they were opposite sides of the same coin.

"If you want, I could go pick up some takeout. Or I make a mean bowl of spaghetti."

"You don't want to take me to a restaurant looking like this?"

"I'd be happy to. Where do you want to go?"

She stopped and turned to him, putting her hands on her slim hips again.

"Doesn't anything ever get you rattled?"

"Only you." He didn't smile.

"Apparently, I'm not very good at it. You never seem to bat an eyelid over anything."

"Batting my eyelids wouldn't be too manly, would it?"

There, she smiled. Phew.

"I could make us an omelet."

"I don't want you to go to any trouble. I didn't come over here so you could cook for me, and I can see that you're not done with that fireplace yet. I could help you out with it."

"The fireplace can wait. It's just a hobby of mine, refinishing things. I like to find stuff that someone has ruined and bring it back to how it was supposed to be."

"I can relate to that. I've done that with some

horses. It makes you wish people hadn't messed them up in the first place."

"Actually, I enjoy the challenge of repairing the damage. I like to think that they come out even better than they were originally." She placed the last rose in the vase and moved them around until they looked balanced. "They're lovely. Thank you."

"You're welcome." Pink roses were perfect for her. Red was too flashy, yellow too noncommittal. Pink to match her cheeks, he was glad he'd made the right choice.

"An omelet will be no trouble. It'll only take a few minutes. I'm really not in the mood to get dressed up, and I think you are fully aware that I would rather die than go to a restaurant looking like this. I think we both called each other's bluff rather well there." She smiled at him. It was actually sweet that he thought she looked cute like this.

"No bluffing on my part. I'll take you out in a garbage bag if you want to wear one. I don't embarrass easily." Jesse leaned lazily against her granite countertop, arms crossed over his chest.

"I'm sure you don't. I do, however. And speaking of which, I'm sorry I passed out the other day. That must have been a little scary for you." Phew. She managed to get that off her chest.

"It wasn't your fault. Don't sweat it. My lovemaking is so incredible that it leaves my lover literally senseless." One side of his mouth curved into a half-smile. He raised a bronzed hand up to the neck of his shirt and reached his fingers inside, rubbing the muscle at the top of his shoulder. Tara felt a disturbing surge of heat rise through her and turned quickly away.

"Don't pat yourself on the back too hard." The open fridge door hid her smile. She was starting to relax again. Somehow Jesse could do that to her, too. She got out the eggs, butter, milk and a head of lettuce, and placed them on the counter.

Without her asking, Jesse came and stood next to her and started pulling the lettuce apart and ripping the leaves into smaller pieces. The nearness of him stirred something inside her. Having him work alongside her in the kitchen felt so intimate, a little unsettling but oddly appealing.

"Have you always lived alone?" she asked him.

"No."

Of course not, what was she thinking? He'd probably lived with a succession of women, each wilder and more beautiful than the last.

"I like living alone." She didn't want him to think she was lonely since Gordon moved out. "I like things done my way, which is easier if you live alone. Don't rip those leaves up so small. They hold the dressing better if you leave a bit of the curve of the leaf."

Jesse paused and looked up at her, raising an eyebrow slightly. "I can see what you mean."

Tara reddened a little. She hadn't meant to illustrate her point quite so vividly. "I'm such a control freak." She cracked the eggs into a bowl. "I'm probably impossible to live with." Maybe she could put him off. He'd go off her sooner or later. Sooner would be better—less likely for her poor, bruised heart to get run through the mangle.

"I don't think you'd be impossible to live with. A bit of a challenge, that's all. Some of us enjoy a challenge. And maybe you need to loosen up and try some new ways of doing things."

"I'm sure I do, I just don't know if I'm capable of it at this point."

"I know you're capable of trying new things. Look at all the new things you've tried since you met me: riding a horse, passing out cold during sex...." He winked at her. "But I'm not going to mess with your salad strategy because I don't have a theory as good as yours and we want those leaves to hold the dressing nicely. Hey, if you know the right way of doing something, there's no harm in saying it."

Most men hated being told what to do. How typical of Jesse to take direction easily. He didn't feel his manhood was at stake because she'd corrected his lettuce-tearing style. Yet she could tell he'd never allow himself to be bossed around. It must be quite something to be that self-assured and yet still be able to get along with others so easily.

She wondered how many others he had gotten along with easily. She couldn't resist asking. "Have you ever had a live-in girlfriend?"

"No." He looked at her steadily, his dark eyes soft. "I'm holding out for the real thing."

Once again she got that funny feeling in the pit of her stomach. Something about Jesse's steady, assured gaze threatened to turn her inside out. *The real thing.* Would she know it if she saw it? She didn't trust herself any more.

Jesse stood and carried the dishes back into the kitchen and she watched him. He moved so confidently, never hesitating. He didn't ask permission, he just did what needed to be done. She picked up their glasses and followed him.

They made coffee and took their cups into her elegantly furnished sitting room. Jesse sat down gingerly on one of the white sofas.

"I hope I don't leave a mark."

"They're Scotchgarded."

"I bet the kids aren't allowed in here." He looked around him at the fine antiques, the authentic Persian rug, the fragile vases and statuettes ornamenting each surface.

"What kids?"

"The imaginary ones that live in those rooms upstairs."

Tara chuckled. "No, I guess this room isn't too kid-friendly, is it?"

"It ain't too grown-up-friendly either. Maybe I'd better take my boots off." He looked down at his boots on the white carpet. He glanced at Tara, who had her bare feet curled up under her as she sat cross-legged on the sofa. "Bare feet look more comfortable anyway."

"Go ahead." Tara looked around her living room as he pulled his boots off. *Living room* was a funny term. It was probably the least-used room in the house. She'd decorated the room as a setting for a fantasy that had almost nothing to do with how she and Gordon had actually lived, and it ended up sitting empty most of the time.

"Can I come sit next to you?"

"Okay." She sipped her coffee. Jesse settled his big body into the sofa next to hers. His upper arm bumped gently against hers, stirring a warm sensation that percolated through her. Her nipples grew firmer just from the nearness of him.

Pheromones, a scientific phenomenon, easily

explained.

He leaned his head toward her and brushed back a strand of hair that was falling over her ear. Then he kissed her ear. A rush of sensation flooded her, and she grabbed at her tilting coffee cup with her other hand.

"Let me take that for you." Jesse removed the cup and placed it on the floor, next to his own. He knelt on the floor in front of her and gently picked up one of her feet, carefully pulling it out from under her and extending her leg toward him.

Looking at her, his eyes slightly narrowed, he slowly lowered his lips right into the curved arch of her foot. As his mouth met the tender skin she felt his tongue dance over the nerve endings concentrated there.

A shudder of pleasure softened Tara and made her fall back against the cushions of the sofa. His mouth followed the line of her foot up to her ankle, then feathered kisses along the smooth length of her bare leg. As he flicked his tongue in the sensitive crook of her knee, he slid a hand up to her crotch and settled his palm over the rapidly heating space between her legs.

Tara willed herself to stay still. She didn't dare respond. If she let herself get drawn into a mutual dance of arousal, who knew where it could lead? She knew she *should* want him to stop—but she didn't.

Oh, Jesse.

His hand slid inside the waistband of her shorts. He raised himself off the floor and moved over her, levering himself into position and slipping his warm, cupped palm right over the hot flesh of her sex.

His fingers moved over the soft silk of her panties,

rubbing, teasing, until her breath came in unsteady gasps.

Don't do it, Tara. Stop this right now. Don't let yourself get carried away.

But she couldn't tell him to stop. It felt too good, too right.

Jesse moved over her, his warm male scent filling her senses, and he dragged his hand over her belly, under her T-shirt and up to her braless breasts. He moaned softly as his fingers touched her hardened nipple, and she released an involuntary gasp.

Lifting her T-shirt, he settled his mouth over her breast and swirled his tongue around her nipple, each time coming closer to the agonizingly tender bead at its center.

Clenching her fingers now, digging into the sofa cushions with her nails, Tara fought against the agonizing waves of desperate need that foamed in her blood.

Don't do it! Don't make love. Don't let him take your control away and leave you unconscious, gone, lost.

But she couldn't make him stop. She couldn't even let the words form on her lips—the lips that parted instantly when Jesse's mouth moved over them, his tongue probing the hot, wordless depths of her hungry mouth.

A traitorous arm shot up from the sofa and grabbed at the back of his neck. An errant leg wrapped itself around Jesse's back as he leaned over her, pushing her into the soft white cushions.

Her other hand sped down his back and inside his jeans, where it grabbed his rear and pulled him toward her. She moaned. Her hands roamed over his back, under and over his shirt, scratching him with her nails, clawing at him in desperation, wanting him, wanting all of him.

She rubbed her face against his, the rough evening beard an agonizingly sweet punishment on her burning skin. She gently bit his cheekbone, sucked at his skin, grazed his neck with her teeth.

Jesse lifted her T-shirt over her head, leaving her bare-breasted, her nipples crimson with arousal as he lowered his face to them, sucking one while rubbing the other with frenzied fingertips. He shook slightly, his desire for her so urgent that he could barely control himself, as he drove her further into a shuddering state of desperation.

He pulled down her shorts and underwear and as his mouth settled over the burning flesh of her crotch, Tara groaned. It was a deep, guttural sound, most unladylike, that came from somewhere deep inside her. Jesse looked up at her, his mouth still working over the painfully aroused crimson flesh of her sex, his eyes black with desire.

As his tongue flicked over her pleasure point, Tara felt a sudden surge of energy. *She had to stop this, and now!* She pushed him off her, fighting him back, a last stand to save herself. He grabbed her wrist and held it. Then their eyes met and at that moment she knew she was lost.

She pushed him down off the sofa and fell on top of him, tugging at his buttons in a frenzied need to feel his flesh against hers. They struggled with the stiff fabric of his jeans, tearing at his boxer shorts until they were both naked on the white rug.

She was burning all over, her center white hot, as she held Jesse deep within her.

The real thing. Was this it? Or was this just the most

intense lust imaginable.

She moved urgently, pushing her hips against him, leading them together in a manic dance, her whole body still quaking with unspent desire. She opened her eyes for a split second and saw Jesse under her, his eyes closed and his face a mask of ecstasy, flushed, openmouthed, hard breaths escaping his parted lips.

Grinding, moving, their shared rhythm pounding in every part of her body, she closed her mouth over his, sucking hungrily while her hands knitted themselves into his hair.

Jesse.

Her hips moved of their own accord as she kissed and licked his face. She could hear herself moaning, their hot breaths mingling as their bodies threatened to explode and destroy what last vestiges of sense and reason they still clung to.

The urgent thrusting of her hips was moving them across the floor, and they reached an obstacle, which she pushed out of the way blindly, with a flailing hand.

Her whole body knew that this was the only man for her. He was hers right now, and he always would be.

She pushed, drawing him deeper inside her, her body on fire with his touch, the deepest touch imaginable.

Jesse.

She heard herself call his name, through the thundering of blood that drummed in her veins. The voice sounded as though it was very far away as she fell heavily onto him, and he wrapped his arms around her so tightly that she knew they could hold her forever and ever.

His arms were still holding her when she opened her eyes. Her head was resting on his chest. She felt his hand stroke her hair as his head lifted to kiss her gently on top of her head.

"You're back." His voice was soft.

"Was I gone long?" She knew she'd lost consciousness again.

"A couple of minutes. But see? You're just fine."

Am I?

8

Tara scrubbed at the carpet again, her elbow sore. Was seltzer supposed to remove coffee stains or was that for red wine? Seltzer certainly wasn't working. The pure New Zealand wool had eagerly welcomed the deep pigmentation from the two cups of coffee she and Jesse had knocked over during their wild tryst.

The Hepplewhite end table she'd shoved over in her frenzy of passion was okay, mercifully, but the little Meissen dog, the closest thing she'd ever had to a pet, had broken in two against the glass candy dish it had shared the table with.

Their postcoital cuddling had been interrupted by the shrill ring of Jesse's phone. One of his horses had been injured by a kick from another horse, and he'd had to leave for an emergency consultation with the vet. He'd carried Tara up to bed first, tucking her in with a kiss, so it wasn't until the harsh light of morning that she'd realized the devastation their careless lovemaking had wrought.

What happened when she and Jesse touched was a train wreck you could see coming. They'd sat there on those sofas, calmly predicting the ruin of the white carpet and the shattering of precious objects. Then they started to kiss, and before they could catch their breath, they were barreling toward the inevitable collision. Now she sat alone in the wreckage.

Her feelings for Jesse scared her. Not just the passing out—though that was alarming enough—but she was growing dangerously attached to him.

This was not good.

He'd lose interest in her sooner or later, probably sooner with all those women coming to him for lessons and training, and she'd be more devastated than ever.

The sound of her phone made her jump. She was tempted not to answer it since she wasn't in any mood for casual chitchat, but the digital display told her it was her mom.

"Hi, Mom." She continued to scrub half-heartedly at the carpet.

"Hi, honey, any news on the TV show?"

"Nothing firm. They want me to come back to L.A. to meet some more people. But, Mom, there's something I've been meaning to ask you." She scrubbed a little harder at the stain, not sure how to formulate what she wanted to say. "Your premature menopause, how did it start?"

She'd been trying not to think about the changes happening in her body, but they were becoming hard to ignore. She was scared and she needed to face the truth of whatever was happening to her.

"Oh, honey, you don't think you're…"

"I don't know. I've been feeling a little odd lately. What kind of symptoms did you have?"

"Gosh, it's hard to remember, it was so long ago. I think I had hot flashes, my periods became irregular and then stopped. I had some headaches. I don't really remember what else."

Oh, no. She had every one of those symptoms. Tara took a deep breath to try and stop the tears welling up in her eyes from spilling. She didn't want her mom to worry.

"Are you having any of those symptoms?"

"Yes."

"Oh, honey. It might be nothing. When did you have your last period?"

"I don't really have periods. I'm on the Pill. But Gordon and I tried to get pregnant for a few months and nothing happened." She'd even done a test after she'd broken up with Gordon. As she'd taken that test she'd held out a bizarre hope that it would be positive, that a baby would somehow be the twist in the tail of the story of their relationship. But she wasn't pregnant, and that was that.

"Maybe the Pill is causing your symptoms. Don't just guess. Go to the doctor."

"I guess I should. I'm scared, though. What if they tell me I can't have children?"

"You've been having hot flashes?"

"Yes." Mostly they happened when she was around Jesse or when he suddenly snuck into her thoughts. But that was hardly surprising, really, that her hormones would get all out of kilter when they were being jump-started by the presence of a man. By the presence of that one man who could always press her buttons without even trying. "What was the reason for your menopause coming early? Did they tell you?"

"Premature ovarian failure. The eggs packing up."

"Is it genetic?"

There was a long pause.

"I'm not sure, exactly." She could hear the sadness in her mom's voice. Her mom knew how much she wanted children. Her mom knew because she had wanted more children herself. So had her father, and now he had them, with his second wife.

"I guess I should go see a doctor."

"Oh, sweetie. You can still have children anyway. You can adopt."

"I know." The tears had started falling now, dripping into the carpet, mingling with the seltzer and the coffee and the matted wool. "I know."

"Don't worry too much until you've talked to a specialist, okay?"

"Okay, Mom. I won't. Can I come over to dinner tonight? It'd be nice to see you. I've been so busy lately."

"Yes, of course! I'll make your favorite, meat loaf."

"Thanks, Mom! I'll pick up some of your favorite pastries from the bakery on my way and see you around five."

She wiped her eyes as she hung up the phone. Phew. At least she would be out of the house tonight, not waiting around to see if Jesse was going to show up again and throw her entire universe off-kilter. She always stayed overnight when she went to visit her mom; it was a ritual, one that they hadn't enacted in quite some time.

And what the heck, some meat loaf and a few apple turnovers weren't going to do any damage that wouldn't be undone by all of those salads she'd be eating in L.A. on her upcoming trip.

What was she going to do about Jesse?

Their relationship was a roller-coaster ride. Exhilarating. Fun. Scary. There were moments when being with Jesse seemed most natural thing in the world, when she was suddenly sure that they were meant to be together. But those moments seemed to come right before she passed out cold. Hardly a good thing!

Any conviction that she and Jesse were perfect together seemed to be a temporary sexual delusion, the result of too many hormones circulating too quickly in her fevered bloodstream.

And afterward, when she regained consciousness—regained consciousness!—she was left wondering what the heck she was doing lying naked in the middle of some totally inappropriate location, the world still spinning around her.

Not natural, and not good.

No. She needed someone who would make her feel…a whole lot less than Jesse made her feel.

If she didn't stop seeing Jesse she was going to have to take out insurance against all the damage that seemed to happen to her possessions when he was around. And it wasn't even his fault. Dating someone who turned you from a mild-mannered decorator into a sex-crazed maniac was not a good thing.

Tara stayed away from his ranch and avoided his texts and phone calls for two days, returning them with a brief, "Be in touch soon." She flew to L.A. for a series of meetings, leaving very detailed instructions for everyone involved in Jesse's project.

When she came back she kept quiet about it for a couple more days, fear still swirling in her heart, but when a big bill came for some furniture she'd had delivered and set up, she couldn't avoid checking it before issuing payment.

As she pulled into the turnaround near the barn she saw Jesse immediately. Her pulse started to pound.

He was talking to a woman, a girl really, probably not more than twenty. She wore riding pants, so presumably she was there for a lesson or to try out a horse. She had long, curly red hair, a big chest and a hearty laugh. Jesse was smiling broadly.

Tara had driven her Porsche, the better for a quick getaway, and she levered herself out of it as gracefully as possible without Jesse's helping hand.

"Hey, Tara!"

"Hello," she said primly.

"Tara, come meet Rebecca, she's going to be the first guest in one of your rooms."

"But they're not even ready yet!" What was he doing, allowing strange women into rooms that she hadn't even inspected? She didn't even pick the sheets yet.

"Oh, all the rooms are just perfect," said Rebecca in a singsong voice. "Jesse showed me them all and let me have my pick." I'll bet he did, thought Tara. The hairs on the back of her neck started to prickle. "I'll be staying here next weekend for a course."

"She liked the Tuscan suite best." Jesse smiled at her. His arms were crossed over his chest.

"I felt like I was back in Siena."

Tara forced a polite smile. "That's the idea. I'm glad you're enjoying it. I really must go check on the rooms. I have no idea what kind of state they're in."

"They look fantastic. The delivery guy had a map of where to put everything, and I oversaw it all." Jesse looked so relaxed it was starting to get on her nerves.

"Oh."

"Rebecca's here to take some lessons from me." Jesse smiled again. Tara felt a prickle of irritation extend right down her spine. She could just imagine what kind of lessons Rebecca might be after. Rebecca's smile when Jesse looked at her was downright proprietary.

"Tara's going to take lessons from me too, aren't you?"

"Yes."

Oops. That wasn't part of her plan, but it slipped out. And it had the desired effect of slightly diminishing the glow of excitement on Rebecca's porcelain-skinned face.

"I can see you're dressed to ride, Tara, so what do you say we have our lesson right now?"

"Okay."

Really? What was wrong with her? She apparently couldn't say no to him. She hadn't worn jeans, but her black stretch pants probably were somewhat appropriate. Rebecca's eyebrows had risen, and Tara felt a sudden surge of adrenaline that Jesse had chosen her over the buxom redhead.

Jesse smiled calmly. "So I'll catch you later, Rebecca, unless you want to hang around and pick up some tips while Tara rides."

Oh, please no. It would be humiliating enough bouncing around like a sack of potatoes on the poor horse. Please don't let anyone else witness it.

"I have some calls to make," Rebecca smiled sweetly. "I'll see you later. Nice to meet you, Tara." The women nodded and smiled politely at each other, and Tara watched Rebecca for a moment as she walked away.

"I thought I was going to have a hard time convincing you to get up on a horse again." Jesse's eyes were sparkling with amusement. His arms were still crossed over his chest, his ubiquitous white shirtsleeves rolled up over his muscled forearms.

"Well, I really should go check on the rooms."

"Hell, no! You said you'd ride and you're riding if I have to throw you over my shoulder and carry you to the arena."

"That won't be necessary."

"Damn, it sounded like fun." He grinned at her. "I've missed you. How was L.A.?"

"Busy. I taped the pilot for a show they're calling *Design in Time*."

"That makes it sound like a race."

"It kind of is. The whole project has to be done over a weekend."

"How come you didn't do all my guest cottages in a weekend? Now that I know what you're capable of, I want some speed."

She lifted a brow. "Rushing a redesign is not my style at all. I believe in taking my time and getting it right. In fact, I'm not sure I'd have flown out there if they'd been up front about the concept. I thought it would focus more on choosing colors."

"But you took a chance and did it anyway." Jesse's dark eyes narrowed a little. When he spoke, his voice was low. "Sometimes it's good to take a risk."

Tara looked at him. "I believe the last time I tried that I ended up naked and unconscious."

Jesse grinned. "Yeah, I remember."

Tara felt a warm core of heat begin to radiate at her center as his mouth twisted into that lopsided grin. She'd probably never said the word *naked* aloud in her life. What was it about Jesse that popped her cork and made her talk and behave, even think, like a different person?

"So am I going to ride a horse or not?"

"You sure are. Let's go get one."

Tara was seated on ChaCha, the same horse she'd ridden on their trail ride. She was absolutely rigid with tension, almost shaking, and even Jesse's soothing words and gentle touches couldn't seem to get her to relax.

"It's important to release the tension, so you can let your body flow with the horse's movements. But don't worry, I have an idea. We're going to get over the hump of anxiety by teaching you how to fall off."

"What?" She knew her eyes were wide with horror.

"You heard me. You're all wound up because you're worried about hitting the dirt at high speed and hurting yourself. I'm going to teach you how to fall off right, so you won't have to worry about it any more."

"That doesn't sound like a good idea at all." Her teeth started to chatter.

"Trust me, I'm an expert." He smiled at her and placed a reassuring hand on her thigh. The warmth of his touch radiated through the thin fabric of her pants. She took a little breath and tried to exhale, then looked doubtfully at the ground, which seemed a very long way away.

"It's just sand, you won't get dirty."

"I'm not worried about getting dirty. I'm worried about breaking my neck."

"I'd never let that happen. Come on, it'll be liberating, trust me." He winked at her. Why did he have to be so damned attractive?

"I don't think I want to be liberated."

"Tell you what, I'll do it first, so you can see how easy it is, okay?"

"Sure." Anything to get off this giant beast. She slid gingerly down out of the saddle, Jesse's hands guiding her gently to the ground.

He climbed up on her horse. He put his feet in the stirrups, which made him look like a jockey since he was so much taller than her.

"All you have to do is kick your feet out of the stirrups, lean forward like this," he inclined himself toward the horse's neck, "drop the reins and roll right off."

In a flash he slid off the horse and hit the ground, where he rolled and landed on his feet. "Nothing to it, see." He held up his arms, as if demonstrating that he was all in one piece. "Ready?" Tara still looked at him doubtfully. "You can try and land on your feet straight off, but it's safer to plan a nice roll. When nothing's rigid, you don't have to worry about anything snapping. Your turn."

"I can't believe you're making me do this."

"You don't want me to think you're a quitter, do you?" He raised an eyebrow.

"I'd rather die." She flashed her eyes at him and he chuckled, causing a low rumble of something deep in her belly. She was starting to feel a bit more relaxed already. And it didn't look like it could kill her.

"That's more like it. Come on, Tara, get up there again." He gave her a leg up.

Following his instructions she dropped her

stirrups, leaned forward, let go of the reins, then…stayed exactly where she was.

"I guess pitching myself onto the ground doesn't come naturally."

"Am I going to have to pull you down?" He put his hands on his hips, and his expression told her he'd be more than happy to do it.

"No, I'll do it right this time."

Once again she got herself into position, and this time she forced herself to slide sideways off the horse and onto the ground, where she found herself sitting, looking up at Jesse.

"Pretty good!" His grin was a nice reward.

"How come I'm not on my feet the way you were?"

"You've got to stand up for that. Here." He extended a hand and helped her up. "Come on, let's do it again. You look more relaxed already."

"You're right. It helps." She shook her head, amazed that she was going through with this. No doubt it would help her grow as a person.

The second time she managed to roll and land on her feet, causing Jesse to clap. A burst of exhilaration tickled her nerve endings. Actually, this was kind of fun!

The third time Jesse was standing a little closer and she dropped down, rolled, landed on her feet and pushed him hard, knocking him to the ground and falling on top of him.

"What the—" He looked so startled that she couldn't help but laugh.

"I don't know what came over me, sorry!"

He grappled her and rolled on top of her. "I'll teach you to knock me down, lady!" He braced his elbows against the ground and Tara tried to fight her way out from underneath him, but her attempts proved totally ineffective. Jesse grinned, and Tara laughed in open mouthed astonishment at her own reckless behavior. She pummeled his chest with her fists.

"Uh-oh, you're starting to get tense again! We don't want that to happen." He narrowed his eyes, "But I think I know one way to soften you up a little."

Suddenly his mouth was on hers, kissing her hard. Her body responded instantly, a rich heat rising through her, her tongue seeking his as her hands wrapped around his back.

Dammit! There was just nothing like kissing this man.

Every nerve in her body burst into flame. There was no way to stop those hot flashes coming on when they came. The touch of his hands on her was like the heating pad her overworked body had been craving.

His arms felt so good wrapped around her, his warm masculine strength enveloping her. She could blame him for pushing her toward the edge, but it was she who jumped every time. She shifted a little and they rolled together until she was on top of him, kissing him with all the passion that had built up inside her during their time apart.

What could she do? She was crazy about him. She kissed his face all over and ran her fingers though his thick hair, sighing at the pleasure of being close enough to smell the heady scent of his skin. His fingers worked on the knots in her spine, softening and loosening, removing every last vestige of resistance as their mouths played over each other licking, tasting, sucking hungrily.

She was hot, feverish with desire, her insides throbbing with need. Jesse groaned, and she could feel his arousal hard underneath her.

"Well, well, you're all relaxed now, aren't you?" His lust-darkened eyes twinkled with amusement. "And much as it pains me, we're not going to let all that softening and loosening of your body go to waste."

"You're not making me get up on that horse again, are you?" With considerable effort she turned to look at ChaCha, who had not moved an inch and was standing watching them as if people did that sort of thing every day in her arena.

"You're damn right I am. C'mon!" He leaped to his feet and pulled her up.

Sure enough, loose-limbed and warmed to the core, Tara had no problem following the motion of the horse.

"You're a natural all right," said Jesse, watching her appreciatively, his hands on his hips. "And you can see the kind of sacrifices I'm willing to make in the pursuit of excellent horsemanship."

Tara had no problem trotting, either sitting to it or rising up and down the way Jesse showed her.

"This is fun!"

"I knew you'd like it. My lady's got to know how to ride a horse."

His words both thrilled and alarmed her. "Your lady? Who says I'm your lady?"

"What, you just push any old guy to the ground and start clawing at him?"

"No." She bit her lip and blushed. What had happened to her resolve to keep herself safe? She could resolve all she wanted when she was alone, but somehow as soon as she was around Jesse, all resolutions went right out the window, taking her good sense with them. She laughed.

"What's so funny?"

"I don't know. I shouldn't be laughing. I'm behaving like a nut."

"You're having a good time."

She looked at him and nodded slowly. "Yes, I am."

"Feels a bit odd, huh?" He tipped his head a little, smiling at her.

"Yes, it does." She shook her head. "I guess I haven't had too much fun lately."

"Don't worry, you'll get used to it. We'll take it slow and build up to genuine enjoyment, so we don't overload your circuits. Will you have lunch with me?"

"Okay."

And they had a nice, quiet lunch in a local restaurant, she looked over the work on the guest houses, and she went home, all without losing consciousness. Maybe there was something to this crazy thing between her and Jesse. Fun, what a concept! There was no denying that it was nice to smile and laugh a little.

9

Tara spent the rest of the day in discussion with TV executives in L.A. A few weeks ago she'd have signed on any dotted line they put in front of her, just to save herself the embarrassment of bankruptcy. Right now, however, she wasn't sure she wanted to move to L.A.

Her hesitation made her bold in her negotiations. She put her foot down on a few points and even managed to negotiate in a clause about using her paint line. And Melody drummed her up a new client. A young couple with a big empty house and a full wallet. She was at her desk at around nine that evening, poring over some blueprints and wondering whether matchsticks really would help keep her eyelids open, when her phone rang.

She didn't recognize the number, but it wasn't Jesse. "Hello." Ugh, she sounded as tired as she felt.

"Ms. Kent?"

"Yes."

"It's Manny, you know, from Jesse West's place." His voice sounded strained.

Tara's pulse quickened. "Hi, Manny, what is it?"

"Jesse's had an accident."

She leaped up from her chair. "What happened? Is

he okay?"

"He was in a car accident. He's a bit shaken up, is all, but he's got to stay in bed for a few days." He paused. "I thought you should know. He didn't ask me to tell you or anything. I don't know if he'd want you to see him laid up in bed and all, but I just…"

"Thanks, Manny, I really appreciate it. I'll be there as soon as I can." She was already grabbing her keys off the side table and hunting around for some shoes. She jumped into her Porsche and sped toward his ranch, playing chicken with the speed limit, her fatigue forgotten.

He must be really badly injured for Manny to have called her. Obviously, Manny knew there was something going on between them. So what? There *was* something going on between them. She hated the idea of Jesse being in pain. She probably should stop off and get some grapes or some soup or something…but she didn't want to waste any time.

She screeched into the turnaround and left her car parked crooked as she walked quickly toward his house. No need to run! If he were really badly injured he'd be in the hospital. Her heart was thudding as she knocked on the door.

"Come in."

What a relief to hear his voice! She barely noticed the cacophony of barking that accompanied her as she walked toward the sound of it, coming from a bedroom in the back of the house.

"Did you decide to give Leader the extra dose?" His voice said through the wall.

"No," she said, as she entered the room. "I didn't."

"Tara! I thought you were Manny."

"I can tell." She smiled, glad to see that he was able to carry on a conversation. He sat in bed, propped up on pillows, surrounded by dogs, cats and papers sprawled over the disarray of sheets and blankets. His face had a nasty purple bruise spreading over one side of it, and his flannel shirt was buttoned wrong.

"What are you doing here?"

"I came to look after you."

"How did you know I need looking after?"

"A little bird told me." She went over and sat on the bed next to him. One of the cats snuck down and slinked away. "That bruise looks nasty."

"Does it? At least my eye hasn't swelled shut. It does throb a bit."

"What happened?"

"A wheel came off my car."

"What? How does that happen?" She moved closer.

"Right now it's a mystery, but the police are investigating. My brother Bowie's convinced it's foul play."

"Someone deliberately trying to hurt you?"

"Or kill me. I guess they forgot that bulls have been trying to kill me for years." He smiled again, then frowned a little. "Smiling hurts."

"Who would try to kill you?"

"Bowie thinks it's something to do with the land we all inherited. Someone who wants to get their hands on it. I'm not so sure. But I'm glad you're here."

"I was worried."

"You must care about me."

"I guess so. Your shirt isn't buttoned right." She

reached forward and started to unbutton it. The undone buttons revealed his heavily bandaged chest. He winced as her fingers moved over it.

She felt her smile disappear from her face. "Oh, my goodness, do you have internal injuries?"

"Cracked ribs. Luckily nothing got punctured."

"Does it hurt?"

"Hurts like hell, and it'll hurt more in a couple of days as I know from past experience."

"Ouch." Tara started to rebutton his shirt, then paused. "How did someone sneak onto your property to tamper with your wheel? Your dogs would have noticed."

"I know. That's what I told the police. They suggested that it could have happened somewhere else. But I told them I hadn't been out except to the feed store and my dad's ranch, and I wasn't at either of those for more than fifteen minutes."

"Fifteen minutes is probably enough. Was your car left unattended at either place?"

"Sure. But at the feed store there was a truck unloading feed bags right next to it the whole time, so nothing could have happened there. I went to my dad's place to meet with the foreman. My brother Bowie is very suspicious of him as he had ties to a girl who was murdered earlier this year. So in some ways he was my number-one suspect—but I was with him the whole time I was there."

"Maybe he had someone else do it. He knew you were coming. Did you tell the police?"

"Sure. But he's slippery as an eel. Has an alibi or a story about everything."

"Very scary." She had goose bumps on her arms. Then she realized it wasn't just fears for Jesse's safety that had put them there. "It's colder in here than it is outdoors."

"It's my first winter in the new house. I haven't got the thermostat thingy figured out yet."

"Where is it?" She shivered, even in her jeans and long-sleeved T-shirt.

"The thermostat is in the kitchen, inside the cabinet above the coffee machine."

She fiddled with it, but couldn't seem to get the digital display to change. She walked back to the bedroom. "Did it come with instructions?"

"Yeah, but one of the cats ate them." Jesse shrugged, then winced, obviously regretting the gesture. "I tried to turn it from air-conditioning to heat, but things seem to have gone in the wrong direction. Help yourself to a sweater from my closet." He indicated it with his head. Then a crooked grin softened his face. "Or on second thoughts come get into bed with me and I'll warm you up."

"Not yet. I'm going to make you dinner. I'll take you up on the sweater, though."

"Do I get a kiss first?" The pleading puppy-dog expression on his face made her smile.

"No," she raised an eyebrow. "You get a kiss after I put the sweater on."

"Fair enough."

Jesse watched Tara while she opened his closet and bent over the shelves near the floor. He was glad he kept his closet so neat. Uh-oh, watching her bend over like that was a sight for sore eyes. And smiling hurt. He tried to keep his smile on the side of his face that hadn't been kissed by the door that afternoon.

"Ah, cashmere, I think I'll wear this one."

"Good choice." *Ouch, don't smile.* He almost couldn't believe that she'd rushed right here. It touched him deeply.

"I see I'm not the only one with a taste for the finer things in life."

"I've always had a taste for the finer things in life, like you." Geez, he sounded kind of pathetic. But maybe it would get him some petting.

"Am I supposed to admire your good taste?"

"I should think so, especially since I showed it at such a tender age."

"Maybe you showed poor taste in liking someone so shallow. I deliberately lost touch with you because I didn't want anyone to know that my life had gone down the drain."

"It's okay. You can make it up to me. Get your butt over here and give me my kiss."

He watched as she pulled the soft cashmere over her head and attempted to fix her hair with her fingers. He patted the mattress next to him and she slid onto the bed.

"I'm afraid to touch you anywhere in case it makes it hurt more."

"Anything that gets touched by you hurts less, believe me."

Tara reached out her long, delicate fingers and delicately touched the side of his face that should have hurt but didn't under her cool touch. Her blue-eyed gaze was a balm she spread on his wounded body. Everything about her was so soft. She was more beautiful than she ever had been when they were both young and foolish.

Her delicate pink lips softly brushed his cheek, which was probably fairly cactuslike at this time of day.

"My lips are softer than my cheek." He winked at her.

"I'll be the judge of that." She hesitated for a moment, then gave him a quick kiss on the lips, pulling away just as his lips reached for hers. "Yes, definitely softer. Did you have dinner?"

"I spent the dinner hour in the emergency room."

"What would you like?"

"Kisses."

"You need protein to rebuild your broken bones."

"I need kisses to rebuild my broken spirit."

"I don't think anything could break your spirit. It's a feisty one."

"Yeah, it's a bit of a bucking bronc. Don't you try and test its breaking point though." He narrowed his eyes at her. "There's a weak spot from where it got cracked by someone. Twice."

"We'd better be careful with it, then. We'll start with a little appetizer kiss." She gave him another quick kiss on the lips. Her lips were so soft, so warm. It was torture to feel them pull away so quickly. "We don't want you to get indigestion."

"Couldn't happen. I can eat like a horse, especially when it's your kisses on the menu." He wondered how much it would hurt to make love with broken ribs. Probably not too bad, right?

"We'll move onto the soup course, then." She leaned toward him and settled her lips gently over his. She licked them once and they parted, allowing her tongue to slip quickly inside and touch his before withdrawing. Jesse felt a little zing of sensual arousal travel from the tip of his tongue, down his spine and right to a certain part of him that was covered by the sheets.

"You're a good cook. I can't wait for the main course."

"Coming right up." She smoothed a stray strand of blonde hair behind her ears and licked her lips. He smiled.

"My tummy's rumbling."

"I can't hear anything." At that moment one of the cats obligingly purred.

"You heard that?" Ouch, that grin wasn't a good idea.

"Yes, it sounds serious. I'll get right on it." And with that she carefully straddled him, taking care not to touch his injured torso, and braced her arms on the bedstead. Her face came closer to his, eyes still open, as her lips settled warmly over his and their tongues began a comforting dance.

Jesse felt no pain at all as Tara's healing draught flooded his body, suffusing his limbs with pleasure and making the blanket move where his erection rose eagerly underneath it.

When Tara pulled back, he opened his eyes and saw her face flushed with desire, her eyes shining and her soft lips moist and slightly parted. He groaned.

"I'm not wearing anything under this blanket, you know."

Tara carefully sat back on his legs, resting her curvy backside on his thighs in a way that made the blanket quiver eagerly.

"I see what you mean."

"He doesn't really care what's going on in the rest of my body. He only knows that you're here."

"Tell him he'll have to wait until your ribs are better." Tara's blue eyes had a serious expression that almost tickled a laugh out of him. "We're not going to risk a compound fracture."

They both looked down at the telltale hump in the blanket.

"He doesn't seem to be listening."

"Perhaps I'll have to have a one-on-one conversation with him."

He saw a hint of mischief in her wide blue eyes before she pulled down the blanket and gave him a healing treatment with her mouth that he knew he'd *never* forget.

Tara hummed as she sautéed garlic and onions for the pasta she was making. Even the onions couldn't make her cry. Jesse brimmed over with grateful adoration for her risqué brand of nursing, and she'd even managed to figure out the thermostat enough to turn off the arctic chill.

Jesse had eased himself painfully out of bed and sat watching her from one of the big chairs around the kitchen table.

"Did I mention that you are perfect?" The cheerful sound of his voice made her smile.

"I believe that was mentioned once or twice in the last five minutes. I thought that being perfect, or trying to be perfect, was my biggest problem, though. I'm beginning to get confused."

"You run into trouble when you try to be all things to all people. That's when you end up shortchanging yourself."

Tara chuckled. "Perhaps I should concentrate on trying to be all things to you?"

"No need for that. You just keep right on being you."

Why did he like her so much? She couldn't figure it out. She didn't even like herself very much a lot of the time.

"I think you still have an idealized image of me. You have your act together a lot better than I do. I think you're much too good for me."

He *was* too good for her. He was too nice, too caring, too generous, too honest. She didn't deserve it, though she could certainly appreciate it.

"Even though I'm still a bit rough around the edges?"

"Your only rough edge is your chin."

Jesse felt his chin thoughtfully. "Not much I can do about that except maybe start shaving twice a day."

"I like a rough edge in the right place. A little texture can be just the thing to enliven a drab surface."

"Are you trying to tell me my surface is drab?"

"Your surface is a bit too colorful now with all that purple, but on the whole I'd say it's very pleasing to the eye."

"I'm glad to hear that. Your surface is very pleasing to the eye, too, but right now I'd prefer to get my hands on it. How long is this dinner going to take?"

"It's ready right now, your majesty."

"Excellent, excellent. Did I mention that you are perfect?"

"I forget."

"I'd better just keep on saying it then."

"Okay."

After dinner Tara tried to convince Jesse that she

needed to go home and finish the work she had been doing earlier, but somehow she ended up in bed with him instead. He'd maneuvered his arm around her shoulders, insisting that the position helped relieve his pain, and Tara didn't have any desire to argue with him.

Their night together had been unexpected, her behavior thoroughly uncharacteristic, and the whole experience perfectly wonderful. Jesse was explaining one of his pet horse-training theories, and Tara was enjoying listening to his homespun philosophies that seemed so much wiser than her own.

"No planning?" Tara sounded skeptical.

"Well, you've got to have a plan, or you won't take that first step. But often the key to achieving your aims is to take your eye off the goal and focus on the journey. Instead of worrying about where you think you should be, just focus on where you are and how to make the best of it. The rest will take care of itself."

"But what's wrong with having a goal and focusing on it? Won't that get you there, too?"

"It might, but then you might be in such a rush to get there that you miss a bunch of crucial steps and end up in the wrong place. Or you might get there and realize that it wasn't the right goal for you."

Tara turned her head to look at him. "In other words, you've got to go with the flow."

Jesse winked at her, smiling. "Follow that river where it takes you."

Tara shook her head slowly. Jesse's smile was infectious, curving her lips up even as she tried to look serious. "That doesn't come naturally to me. I'm much happier trying to plan a bridge over the flow in happy anticipation of the firm footing on the other side."

Jesse raised an eyebrow. "How do you know it ain't quicksand on the other side?"

Tara looked at him thoughtfully. "I've been stuck in quicksand for the last eight years, and I'm just starting to feel like there might be a way out."

"Take my hand, I'll pull you free. Though we might have to wait until my ribs heal up a bit and I get my strength back. We don't want me to fall in there with you."

"Oh, I don't know. It might be fun. Go with the flow, right?" She raised an eyebrow at him.

He nodded. "Now you're really getting it." His dark eyes were shining with amusement and anticipation of spending a long night stuck in metaphorical quicksand with Tara. "Stop talking and bring those lips over here."

And they exchanged words for kisses, flowing just a little bit further together up the rapid-churned river of their renewed relationship.

Tara almost asked Jesse what he was doing for Christmas, only two days away. But that might have involved revealing that she was currently doomed to spend it alone, possibly watching The Princess Bride on DVD for the eighty-seventh time. Her mom had already left for Arizona, and Melody was spending Christmas in Vegas with her new husband, in the house she and Tara had designed. She decided it was safer to just keep quiet about her sad and lonely state.

The next morning Melody called and pried the previous evening's events out of her. "My, my, this does sound promising." Tara could hear Melody's spoon clinking around inside her teacup at the other end of the phone line. "There's nothing like a minor injury to bring out your inner Florence Nightingale. He probably planned it on purpose."

"If everyone had the base motives you attribute to them, Melody, the world would be a very frightening place."

"The world *is* a very frightening place, darling. Just ask my first three husbands."

"I'd rather not. Do you really think there could be a future for us?" The question had been weighing on her mind. She'd tried to dismiss Jesse as an impossibility, but he just wouldn't be dismissed. She liked him. He liked her. Maybe she and Jesse weren't such a crazy mismatch after all.

"Why not? Are you holding out for a pinstriped chinless wonder with a busy law practice, not a burly horse trainer?"

"You have such a way with words, Melody. I do worry that he'd get bored with me. I don't know anything about horses."

"So what? My first husband was a down-home Texan who called me y'all even when we were alone in bed together. Of course his money was a consolation. Jesse West's cowboy boots are very well-heeled from what I hear, so you can put up with a few rustic quirks in the reassuring certainty that you won't leave the relationship empty-handed."

"Melody! I honestly don't know how we've managed to stay friends this long. I really should hate you. I'm already getting back on my feet and making my own money so I'm not looking for someone to fleece either. I just don't want to get all excited and happy, then get my heart crushed again."

"You're so simple and innocent, Tara. You really do deserve to be happy."

"Do I? Ever since the Gordon debacle I've been frightened by my capacity for self-delusion. What was I thinking, getting back together with him and letting him string me along for another two years? Am I kidding myself that Jesse and I could actually be a thing?"

"For ever and ever?"

She hesitated. For ever and ever. That was a long time. The idea of spending a long time with Jesse sounded good. The idea of waking with him every morning, of settling down with him every night. She'd been letting her mind play with the idea, and it gave her a warm feeling that was very unfamiliar but undeniably appealing.

"Well, sweetie, there's one good way to find out."

The ugly thought that had been bothering her on and off for a few weeks now pushed its way to the forefront of her consciousness.

"I think I'm going through menopause early."

"What nonsense."

"No, really. My mom had premature menopause. She couldn't have any more children after me. I'm having the same symptoms—hot flashes, crazy moods. I tried to get pregnant with Gordon and it didn't happen."

There was a pause. Tara could almost hear Melody digesting the information, making calculations. She didn't think it was nonsense any more.

"You need to see a specialist."

"I've already made an appointment. They're making me wait for it, but he's supposed to be the best in Austin."

"Good. But seriously, darling, if Jesse had been desperate to have children he probably would have had some by now. He hasn't any, has he?"

"No."

"So he probably doesn't care all that much about them. He's got his horses to fuss over. Don't worry too much, okay, Tara? I want you to be happy, and from everything I've heard he's a lovely man. Who cares if doesn't fit some silly image you had in your mind. Happiness is a rare commodity. Even if it doesn't last for ever you should grab it and hold on to it when you can get it."

Tara sighed. "I think you're right, but I don't trust what I think any more."

"Then trust what I think."

"But you've been married three times. Four now! I'm losing count."

"We're all just guessing here; there's no rule book to follow."

"Ain't that the truth," said Tara slowly. She took a big bite out of the chocolate bar she had just unwrapped and chewed it contemplatively.

10

It was Christmas day, and Tara stood on the scale, her mouth hanging open in disbelief.

"Five pounds? How is it possible to gain five pounds in two weeks?" She'd eaten out a few times, but this was ridiculous.

And she was talking aloud to herself. Fat *and* crazy. "When did I last weigh myself?" She couldn't remember. It had probably been a while. Maybe these five pounds had been sneaking up on her all winter.

She'd been too busy to go running, that was the problem. It was time for drastic action. The Princess Bride could wait. She wasn't going to stop exercising until she'd lost all five pounds. Well, not until she'd had a good, solid workout, anyway.

She rifled through her drawers for her tightest workout gear. Shorts and a T-shirt weren't going to cut it today. She needed to see every one of those five pounds outlined and highlighted in colorful high-tech fabric.

She found a sports bra and matching stretch capris in a shade of baby blue that complemented her eyes and added several square feet to her silhouette.

"Moooooo," she said to her reflection in the mirror. She needed motivation. Her energy level was low, but that was hardly surprising since she'd been putting together a proposal since at least one hour before dawn.

She surveyed the pale-blue apparition in front of her. Most of the weight seemed to have settled into her now ample thighs from the looks of it. When she stood up straight, they were actually touching. Her waistline was in danger of disappearing altogether, and if she wasn't mistaken her breasts had put on a cup size as well.

She wasn't in the mood for running, though. She pulled up a workout video on her big-screen TV and attempted to do some stretches along with the perky instructor.

Lord, she was tired.

"You're falling apart!" She shouted at herself. It didn't help much, but she kept trying to wave her arms in the air in time with the music. Lying down on the couch seemed a much better idea. She was getting breathless, and they hadn't even gotten to the aerobics section yet.

The doorbell rang. She froze. Who would ring the doorbell on Christmas day? Wasn't everyone at home eating turkey with their loved ones and trying on unflattering gifts before burying them in the back of their closets?

Maybe she could pretend no one was home. That would be better than being discovered alone at Christmas, like a total loser.

The bell rang again.

Damn. Did Fed Ex deliver on holidays? She was waiting for some new wood stain she'd ordered for her fireplace. She could always make up some story about how she was exercising before going out to eat a huge dinner. Yes. That would work. She paused the video and went to open the door.

"Hi, Tara." It was Jesse, half concealed by a beautiful bouquet of flowers in a glass vase.

"Jesse!" Her heart started beating faster and she could feel a smile spreading across her face. "Are you supposed to be up and about?"

"There's no keeping me down. Can I come in?"

Tara remembered her hideous pale blue ensemble and the way it enhanced the expanded acreage of her body. She pulled the door open and stepped behind it, hoping to conceal herself. Maybe she could sidestep from there to the hall closet and grab some kind of cover-up.

"Are you going to come out from behind that door so I can give you a kiss? I bought flowers already in a jar so you wouldn't have to do all that snipping stuff." He put the vase down on the table in the foyer and held out his arms. There was nothing for it but to step into them.

And it felt so good. Jesse's arms encircled her and held her against his chest. "I missed you," she said into his shirt.

"Not as much as I missed you."

"What is this, a competition?" She looked up at him. His brown eyes were soft with an expression she hadn't seen before: a gentle and hesitant look.

Her eyes closed as their lips came together and their mouths welcomed each other. Her heart fluttered happily in her chest as she held Jesse tightly. For now it didn't even matter that he'd found her alone on Christmas day. "I thought you'd be spending the day with your family?"

"I was suppose to drive up to my brother Daniel's

place in the mountains, along with Bowie and Lucy, but I didn't think my broken ribs would enjoy that much time sitting in a car, or bouncing up the rocky dirt road to his house. I hoped you'd be home."

"I am. However, I'm afraid that despite the gaudy decorations outside I don't have even one Christmassy thing to eat or drink. I was rather pretending that Christmas wasn't happening this year."

"Works for me. Let's pretend it's Valentine's day instead." And he kissed her so tenderly that she lost all track of time and place.

When they finally parted, Jesse stepped back and appraised her pale blue ensemble. He let out a low whistle.

She cringed. "I was trying to do an exercise video. I'm sure I look really scary."

"You look good enough to eat."

"I've gained weight."

"In all the right places." That familiar crooked grin had spread across his face and he couldn't seem to take his eyes off her body, especially her newly broadened hips. Tara wanted to curl up and hide. It was one thing for her to know she had gained weight, and quite another for him to actually say that he could see it.

He placed a broad hand on the curve of her hip and squeezed slightly.

"Yes, I'm sure you can pinch more than an inch," said Tara, feeling her face color.

"I'm not trying to pinch anything," said Jesse through his grin, "just feeling it up a little. And it feels good." He slid his hand up to her waist, or at least where her waist used to be, then slipped the other hand around it and pulled her until her soft belly was touching his flat one. "If I wanted to fondle a rock-hard body I'd sleep with a man. These curves are the stuff dreams are made of."

"It's nice of you to be so polite about it."

Hmm, she was starting to feel a little sexy.

"Polite? That's not what I'd call the way I'm ogling you. I just can't seem to stop myself." He pulled her away from him a little and sneaked another peek down at her full thighs. "Hot damn!" He shook his head and exhaled audibly.

Oh, well, maybe gaining five pounds wasn't such a bad thing after all! Come to think of it, she was a little hungry right now.

"Would you like some decaf? Caffeine doesn't seem to agree with me lately." It had a tendency to bring on one of those depressing hot flashes, but she wasn't going to tell him that. She cut them each a large slice of chocolate cheesecake. Why the heck not?

"Decaf is fine. You look like you want to ask me something."

"Am I that transparent?" There was a question that had been hovering in the forefront of her consciousness lately. Perhaps Jesse's comment was a sign that now was the right time to ask it.

"You know that I was in a long relationship that just ended. I'm sure that you must have had a serious relationship before now, even if you were traveling a lot. I don't mean to pry. I guess I just want to know more about you."

There, she'd said it. It wasn't natural for a man to be single at thirty and never have had a girlfriend. If there hadn't been one, she wanted to know why.

"That's okay. I did have a girlfriend."

Tara's heart started to pound a little. She wanted to know but at the same time she didn't want to know.

"For how long?"

"Four years."

"Was it serious?"

"As serious as it could be with me traveling all over for the rodeo. But she didn't want to have kids, and I just couldn't seem to get past that."

Tara felt her stomach drop. All the blood seemed to drain from her body, leaving her limp and lifeless. Her chocolate cheesecake suddenly tasted like rusty nails.

"Why didn't she want any?" Her voice shook a little.

"She was a serious barrel racer, very competitive. She didn't want anything to interfere with her training and competing. I could understand her point of view, and I tried to be sympathetic to it."

"But?" She raised her cup of coffee to her lips, hoping that he wouldn't see them tremble.

"I really want to be a dad." He smiled. "I've always wanted to be a dad. And not just one kid, I want lots of them. I loved having three brothers to play with. And now that I have my ranch all built up I can't help picturing a whole bunch of kids running around, riding the horses, climbing the trees, livening the place up a bit."

While he was talking, leaning back in his chair and looking cheerfully ahead to the prospect of raising a large brood, Tara felt her heart sink lower and lower inside her rapidly deflating chest.

She could relate to what Jesse was saying. She'd always pictured herself with two children, or maybe three, reading them stories, taking them to the zoo and the circus, making cupcakes and shaped cookies with them.

"I tried to tell myself that having children was just something that either happened or didn't happen," he continued, "that it was our life together that was important. But somehow I never really believed it."

He broke up with his ex because she didn't want children. Would he break up with her because she couldn't give him any?

Perhaps she could pretend she wasn't sure she wanted any and feel him out from that angle. She didn't want him to know that she didn't even have a choice in the matter. That her body was already announcing that its childbearing days were over.

"Do you think it's unnatural for a woman not to want children?"

"I think not wanting kids is fine for some people. But I guess none of those people is the woman for me. Now, the kind of woman who has bedrooms all ready for a boy and a girl she hasn't even had yet," he winked at her, "that's the kind of woman I'm looking for."

He leaned forward and forked a piece of cheesecake into his mouth, watching Tara while he chewed it. His eyes were smiling. He obviously assumed that she totally agreed with him and would be pleased to hear about his paternal ambitions. She covered her confusion with a succession of coffee sips.

Uh-oh, was he overdoing it again? She looked a little on edge. He was so excited to finally have her within reach that he just wanted to run to a church and charge down the aisle with her and get on with building their future together.

He wasn't a very skilled suitor. He hadn't had much practice. Usually women were coming after him hell for leather and all he had to do was fight off the ones he wasn't interested in. Tara was quite a different story.

She was interested in him. He figured they'd established that clearly. But everything after that was still a bunch of balls up in the air. If he played them carefully, they'd come right down into his hands and he'd be carrying her over the threshold on the way to happy-ever-after. If he fumbled them…well, he would have blown his third chance with her and he knew there wasn't going to be another.

She had another one of those big questions forming in her head. He could see it. Being able to read people's body language was definitely a mixed blessing.

"What's on your mind?"

"How do you know there's anything on my mind?"

"I'm a mind reader, remember?"

"Oh, yeah, that." Her attempt at a smile was not very convincing. "Then you'll know that I'm trying to decide whether reclaimed wide pine or hand-chiseled oak floors will work best in the apartment I'm designing."

"No, you're not." Was she wondering about his ex-girlfriend? Whether he still liked her? He didn't. He'd all but forgotten her the moment they broke up, but he wasn't sure if that information would be reassuring or not.

"Was your ex-girlfriend younger than you?"

He shrugged. "I guess so. By three years. Why do you ask?"

"My father cheated on my mother with a woman fifteen years younger than him. My ex-fiancée's new arm candy is barely out of college. Let's face it, men like them young, preferably young and stupid." Her face reddened, and she quickly picked up her coffee cup and took a sip.

"It doesn't matter who I've dated in the past or how old they were. I've never felt anything for one of them that could hold a candle to what I feel for you."

"You barely know me!" She was shaking her head.

"I've known you half my life," he said softly. Even when they were apart he knew that he'd carried a little piece of her with him.

"Not really." Tara sat back in her chair. Her brow wrinkled slightly. "We were just friends back at school."

"But we both felt the connection between us, didn't we?" He watched as she looked down into her coffee cup. "Go on, admit it. That kiss didn't come right out of the blue."

He'd dreamed about that night long before it happened. He didn't know how it was going to happen, or when, but he knew that he and Tara Kent were destined to come together.

"No," she looked up at him with those wide blue eyes. "It didn't come out of the blue. There was something about you that attracted me." She tilted her head to the side as she spoke, a twinkle of approval lighting her eyes. "It's not something I can define. I felt it again as soon as we met. There's something about you."

"Apart from my rugged good looks?"

"Apart from those, yes." She smiled. Her smile was always like the sun coming out from behind a cloud. "So what did you see in me that got you so interested?"

"I think every boy in the school had a crush on you. You were smart, beautiful, nice, popular, what's not to like?"

"That's pedestrian stuff. Is that really what attracted you to me?"

"No." He shook his head. "I just knew that you were the one for me."

"You must have been disappointed when you realized I wasn't the woman of your dreams."

Jesse laughed. "Hell, I was disappointed to realize that I wasn't the man of your dreams, but you've always been the woman of my dreams. You still are."

He looked at her. It was amazing how little she'd changed in their years apart. She had tiny laugh lines around her eyes that made her more beautiful and radiant than ever.

"I don't think any woman can live up to a dream." She looked down into her coffee cup.

"A dream is a pale and insubstantial thing compared to a real flesh-and-blood woman." He reached out and placed his hand over hers. Her eyes flashed up to him. When they touched that magic always lit up between them. He knew she could feel it, too.

He rose from his chair, still holding her hand, and moved around the table. He raised her to her feet and kissed her gently on the lips.

"I don't want to scare you off, Tara, lord knows." He looked at her lovely face, her lips parted, slightly moistened by their kiss. "But I don't think I can go much longer without telling you…" He kissed her softly again on those seductive lips. "There's just no easy way to put it…" Her brow wrinkled softly, wondering what he was going to say. There was a mild look of alarm in the calm blue of her eyes.

"I love you, Tara. I just love you. I can't help myself." There, he'd said it. He'd tried not to, but it just came out. Hell, he'd been waiting twelve years to say it.

He looked at those blue eyes and saw the tears gathering in the corners, drops building and spilling out over her lashes.

"Don't cry, Tara. It's okay if you don't love me. Just give us time. Give us the chance to get to know each other slowly. Give us the chance we didn't have all those years ago."

Two fat tears ran parallel over her pink cheeks. He reached up a thumb and brushed one of them aside. He kissed the other tear away, and its salt taste lingered on his lips.

He didn't like to see her cry. After she cried, then she left, and she didn't come back. But last time she'd cried he'd gone after her, and here they still were, together. He wasn't going to let her get away this time.

"You're too good for me, Jesse. I'll never be the woman you think I am." Two more tears fell as she blinked. He let them fall.

"Just be the woman you are. That will always be enough for me."

She bit her lip and looked away. She didn't believe him. But he'd show her, little by little, day by day, year by year, that he was telling the truth. If she'd give him the chance.

"You look tired. Why don't we take you upstairs and tuck you into bed?"

"That sounds good." She wiped the tears from her eyes with a hand.

Jesse led the way to her bedroom, holding her hand. Together they walked past that silent little boy's room with its teddy-bear cowboys riding over the empty bed, and the pink girl's bedroom, its painted roses twining around an empty crib. He'd make her dreams come true, if she'd only let him.

"Let's get that foxy blue outfit off you."

"All right." She smiled, that golden ray of sunshine illuminating her face. As he slid her sports bra up over her head, he kissed her breasts and belly, sighing at the wonderful softness and warmth of her lovely body.

He paused just below her belly button, inhaling her scent as he stroked the curving outline of her hips. Ah, heaven!

But she was tired. Heaven could wait.

He slipped her tights down past her ankles and she stepped out of them and hopped quickly under the covers of the bed. Jesse swiftly peeled off his clothes and climbed in with her.

"I thought you were going to tuck me in?"

"On second thoughts I think you need a teddy bear to cuddle."

"And you're going to be my teddy bear," she smiled, her head resting on the pillow.

"Just like in the song."

When Tara awoke Jesse was sleeping, one arm behind his head, the muscled brown curves of his body outlined against the white sheets in the pale half-light of the moon.

She looked at him, studying his face in a way she'd never felt able to do when he was awake. She could see the imperfections that were hidden when his face was animated, the scar along the ridge of his chin, the slight crookedness to his nose betraying an old break, the roughness of his tanned skin caused by overexposure to the sun.

He wasn't perfect. He wasn't even pretending to be. He was living his life according to his principles and assuming that others would do the same. He was a simple man, really, much simpler than her.

He didn't seem to worry about who he wasn't and who he should be, he just was. He didn't get all tangled up in trying to convince anyone that he was flawless and invincible. Why did it gall her so much to admit her own failings?

It was comforting to think that even if you knew your life was a mess, everyone else thought it was an ideal to aspire to. But that illusion was shot ever since Gordon dumped her anyway. Now she was just another single woman with her biological clock ticking loud enough to wake the dead.

Funny thing to be thinking when there was a sleeping man in your bed.

She wasn't really single. She had a man. There he was, head resting on her pillow. Why didn't it feel real? Was it too good to be true?

She allowed a smile to play across her lips as she looked at Jesse's sleeping form. The duvet cover had become bunched under him, revealing one side of his body. She let her eyes wander from the elbow crooked behind his handsome head, down past the dark hollow of his armpit to his muscled torso, its center shadowed with black hair, sliding past a slim hip and down one long, sturdy leg. From this angle she couldn't see any bruising from his accident.

She could admit to being seduced by his very masculine beauty, its flaws adding texture and liveliness to the whole. His lips were closed, and his mouth curved very slightly into the faintest hint of a smile.

"You'd better be dreaming about me," she whispered.

His shadowy smile deepened. "You know you're the woman of my dreams," he said softly, sleepily. His eyes cracked open slightly, the reflection of the moon lighting their darkness. "I'm pretty sure I'm still dreaming, but it's a good one."

Tara leaned over him and kissed him gently on the lips.

"And it just got even better," he said huskily.

She lowered her mouth over his again and licked his lips until they parted. Their kiss was soft, slow, the gentlest of awakenings. Tara enjoyed the beginnings of a warm fire deep inside her, not one of those searing hot flashes, but a comforting glow that spread throughout her limbs.

Their bodies settled together comfortably, fitting each other like a matching pair as their hands began to slowly roam over the warm, relaxed flesh of the other.

"Mmm, this is one heck of a way to wake up," Jesse murmured in her ear, as her fingertips slid along the hollow of his spine. He kissed the soft flesh of her earlobe and then sucked it gently. Tara ran her fingers over the hard ridges of muscle on his back, sighing at the wave of pleasure that rose within her.

Their lips met in a sensual kiss as their bodies nestled together. Tara felt her nipples growing hard against his firm pectorals. Jesse's hand slid down her back, over her buttock and thigh, and into the soft, wet place between her legs.

"I see you're preparing a warm welcome for me," he whispered softly. Tara felt a smile creep across her face, her cheeks heated with the passion simmering inside her.

"Come on in, the water's lovely," she heard herself say, her voice sultry with desire, as she pressed her thighs against his, rubbing her hands over the firm curve of his backside. Jesse eased himself on top of her and entered her effortlessly.

Ohhhh. She wasn't sure if she said it aloud but the sigh of relief came from every cell in her body. It was good to have Jesse deep inside her.

He moved over her gently, filling her, making her moan softly. Her skin tingled with the glory of touching him. Her whole body glowed with delight, and she was sure that if she opened her eyes they would both be shimmering iridescent in the moonlight.

He had said he loved her.

I love you. The words echoed in her mind.

I can't help myself.

Was that how love was? It just took hold of you and told you what to do, regardless of whether it was the sensible thing or not?

His mouth was teasing along the sensitive skin of her neck while he thrust gently deeper and deeper into the molten core of her body. She felt herself slipping, losing her grasp on reality with each thrust as he dove further inside her and her body opened to receive him.

"Jesse," she moaned aloud, wanting to name him, to say the name of her lover.

I love you. Her mind thought it, but her mouth didn't say it. She hadn't drifted that far away from that rigid core of "good sense" inside her that kept a tight grip on her emotions.

Images grew inside her head, sudden flashes of premonition, like memories that hadn't happened yet. With each thrust of his hard maleness into her soft, female center she saw a glimpse of their future. She saw herself and Jesse living together, laughing together, waking together each morning for the rest of their lives. She saw them walking, talking, playing with their children, growing old together.

She raised her hips under him, closing whatever infinitesimal distance was left between them. They were destined to be together, even all those years ago. Their coming together had been delayed by her foolishness, but it was inevitable.

He was her mate.

The images floated up in her consciousness and popped like bubbles as her body rose under Jesse's, giving herself to him, wanting to join with him in every way, wanting to be one with him. She wanted to share her future with him, she wanted to give him children and…

Then she remembered.

She couldn't give him children.

She was a hollow shell that looked like a woman on the outside, but inside was empty, dark, cold, the doors shuttered against life and hope.

She sank back into the mattress. Jesse's body followed her, still easing himself in and out of her, kissing her face. In spite of her mind her body blossomed under his loving touch. Ignorant of its infertility her womb responded to him, sending out heat waves of desire that suffused her limbs.

Her arms and legs wrapped around her lover, pulling him toward her, inhaling the intoxicating scent of him, filling herself with him. *Jesse, I love you.* The thoughts gathered in her head, then dissipated like clouds. She could feel the heat inside her building toward an inevitable conflagration.

She clutched at Jesse, holding him against herself, her need for him overriding any thought process. She shoved her hips against his, their bellies touching as she moved in rhythm with him. Jesse groaned, moving faster, and she felt the first wave of small contractions beginning in her deep inner muscles.

It was coming. She was barreling forward toward the edge of that cliff. She clung to him and he to her, arms wrapped around each other, holding on for dear life. His breath heated her ear as he moaned her name.

"I love you," he gasped, losing control, shuddering and burying his face in her neck.

I love you, responded her whole body, waves of sensation rising through her as her body rushed to join Jesse in the calm after the storm.

No! No! No!

She snapped herself back from that cliff edge.

"No!" She shouted, her eyes popping open. "No!" She couldn't go there. She couldn't head over that precipice into the black depths of the unconsciousness that waited there for her.

Jesse's eyes opened, the moon a silver coin in the middle of their blackness.

"Don't be afraid, Tara." His voice was breathless but soft with kindness. His hand stroked her hair. "It's okay, I'll look after you."

"I can't." Her body was quivering, craving its own ecstatic release, but her mind held it back. "Hold me." She closed her eyes tight, willing herself back away from the edge.

Jesse wrapped his arms tighter around her. The heavy weight of his body soothed and softened hers. As he stroked her hair and whispered in her ear, gradually the tension drained from her body.

"You don't have to be afraid to let go," said Jesse softly. "I'll always pick you up when you fall."

Tara felt the slightest smile tease her lips up at the corners. "Knowing you you'll even teach me how to fall right."

"If you'll let me. Merry Christmas, beautiful."

"Merry Christmas, Jesse." And it was merry. Merrier than she'd dared to imagine was possible.

11

Jesse invited Tara for dinner the following week to celebrate the completion of his guest cottages. He handed her a big fat check, and they ate his homemade lasagna. After he cut the cheesecake and brought them both slices, he unfurled a big sheaf of papers.

Tara peered at them. "Your blueprints?" They were the architect's drawings for the house they were sitting in.

"I'd like to hire you to finish it out properly."

"But it's already lovely." She gestured around at the cool, masculine decor. Sure, she could liven it up with some textures and art, but— "What did you have in mind?"

Jesse looked at her for a moment as if the answer to that question should be blatantly obvious. "I need the bedrooms decorated. For the cats. Three more of them showed up."

"Oh." Tara smiled. One of Jesse's feline friends brushed up against her leg, and she reached a hand down to stroke it.

"And this big back room is supposed to be a formal dining room, but I never use it. I'd like to turn it into a studio." His big fingertip pressed into the paper.

"What do you want a studio for?"

"It's not for me, really. It's for my wife. I expect I'll marry one of those artistic types." He looked at Tara, his dark eyes dancing with amusement but his face serious.

Heart pounding, Tara raised an eyebrow. "Do your cats really need three bedrooms? I know none of them are for the dogs, since they follow you from room to room and would hate the prospect of having to be separated from you by a wall."

"Do my dogs bother you?" He looked genuinely concerned.

"No, I think they're sweet." She glanced at them where they lay curled up on the floor, adoring eyes never far from their beloved master. "It must be nice being worshipped like that."

"You should know." His steady, confident gaze never wavered. Unfamiliar emotion flared in her chest. She wasn't used to being...cherished. It felt wonderful.

"Anyway," he continued, "the cats can get their asses down to the barn if they want more space, that's where they earn their keep anyway. The three bedrooms are for my kids." He looked at her shyly.

Oh, dear. She knew it was coming, but she still felt like she'd been punched in the gut.

"You're going to have three?" She tried to keep her voice from shaking.

"Three's a nice number, don't you think?"

"It sounds like you have it all figured out." She swallowed hard as a sudden surge of un-nameable emotion threatened to engulf her. "Have you decided whether they are going to be boys or girls yet?"

"Doesn't matter to me. I'll be happy with whatever I get. I've waited a long time to have kids."

You'll be waiting a whole lot longer if it's me you're planning to have them with. Her pulse hammered at her temples, and a wave of nausea rose through her. Jesse was smiling, obviously enjoying the vision of three little tykes tearing around his beautiful new house.

The way he spoke he seemed to think that the whole thing was a done deal. He had their future all mapped out like these crisp blueprints, all he had to do was whip out a credit card and make it happen.

She wanted to cry.

"Why stop at three? Why not have five, or six, or more?" She heard her voice rise and she could feel a flush creeping up her neck.

"Sounds good to me." Jesse grinned. He was so caught up in his rose-tinted vision of the future that he didn't seem to notice that she wasn't gazing through the pink glasses with him. "I always thought it would be fun to have a big family. That's why I built such a big house. It needs finishing though. We'll need storage for all the toys kids have these days. I think it'll be fun to spoil 'em."

Her pulse hammered in her temples. She had to let him know that she could never give him the family he wanted.

How would he react?

Would his face reveal his dismay? She suspected it would.

He was too nice to simply tell her it was over. He'd try to let her down gently. He'd ask her over a few more times and let things cool off in a way that would seem natural, then after a few days apart he just wouldn't call her and she wouldn't call him and it would be over.

It would all be over.

Her last relationship had ended up in the dumpster, even after eight long years of dreaming, planning and hoping.

But she didn't want him to remember her as someone who no one would ever want.

If they had to go their separate ways, she'd prefer him to remember her the way she was in his imagination, the way she'd been when she was younger. Confident, breezy, ready to take on the world. He wanted him to look back at her and sigh wistfully over unattainable Tara Kent, the one who got away.

Tara sat back in her chair, scraping it loudly away from the table and settling her hands primly in her lap. "Jesse. You're a nice man, but if this vision of family happiness includes me, then I'm afraid it isn't going to happen."

Jesse's contemplative smile turned into a small frown. "I know it seems soon. I don't want to rush you, but it just doesn't make sense to delay the inevitable. You know as well as I do that we're meant to be together, Tara."

"I don't know anything of the kind. I've enjoyed the time I've spent with you. It's been fun, at least the parts that I was conscious for." She raised her eyebrows. "But I've never for a moment thought that it could be anything more than a temporary affair."

"I don't believe that. I know that you've felt something for me. I…" He paused, looking at her intently, trying to read something in her expressionless face.

A poker face was one of her most reliable assets. If

she focused completely on keeping her features absolutely calm, on not moving one muscle or betraying even a smidgeon of emotion, she could get through this.

"I know you've been frank with me about your feelings," she said coolly.

When you told me you loved me.

Her heart clenched, and she prayed that she could hold herself together a little longer. "And I should have said something earlier. I feel rather as though I've led you astray."

She'd never told him that she loved him. She'd never betrayed feelings that could be attributed to anything deeper than lust. There was a lot to be said for being emotionally repressed.

Her voice sounded icy. She could even hear a little of the fake Boston Brahmin accent she'd cultivated creeping in there to hide her Texan twang when she was in boarding school. Let him think she was pretentious and shallow. She was.

Jesse tipped his head, still trying to read her. His expression looked doubtful. He didn't believe her. She was going to have to up the ante.

"When the show goes into production, I'll be moving to L.A." She hadn't heard a word about whether it was even happening, but it was a good excuse. One he'd believe.

A muscle twitched in Jesse's cheek. Now he believed her.

"But you can't—"

"Of course I can." She forced a tinny laugh. "You think that after finally getting my business back on its feet, I'd let a fling with an animal trainer interfere with my plans?"

"A fling with an animal trainer? You make it sound like the circus was in town and you've been getting it on with a handsome lion tamer, but you aren't going to follow them to the next city." He looked at her with disbelief.

"Well, that's about the size of it. I'm sorry if you think I've led you on. I really didn't intend to."

Jesse stared at her, his mind obviously working. "No, I don't suppose you did." He was probably racking his brain for sweet nothings she had said to him, or times when she had initiated their encounters. She was confident that he would come up empty-handed. She was used to hiding her feelings, keeping her true thoughts under wraps. It was safer that way.

A deafening crash of thunder sounded over the house, followed almost immediately by a flash of lightening that momentarily illuminated the room and highlighted the stunned expression on Jesse's face.

Tara felt a terrible weight of guilt and sorrow descend on her as the sudden downfall of heavy rain pounded against the roof and windows of Jesse's beautiful house. But she kept her poker face firmly in place.

It was a shame that his big dreams couldn't come to fruition. It would have been nice to live here with him and all his crazy animals, even if they didn't have children.

Don't think about it. Just focus on letting him down and getting out of here before you weaken and tell him the real reason why you'll never be good enough for him. Before he finds out how worthless and empty you really are.

He'll get over you, he did before.

Would she get over him? It didn't really matter. She'd managed to claw her career back from the dead.

Even if the show didn't pan out, she was making enough to pay the mortgage on the house until it sold. Talk about the TV show had soothed the paint manufacturers, and they'd put a hold on the lawsuit. Maybe she would move to L.A. and buy a house on the beach and start a new life. Maybe she'd even get a dog or a cat.

A terrible weight of fatigue descended on her. She rested a hand on the table, bracing herself against it.

"Oh, Tara, I know you don't mean it." Jesse's voice was rough with raw emotion. He was reading her and seeing the truth. *Quick, batten down the hatches!* She straightened her back.

"I want to spend the rest of my life with you." He said it so softly. His brown eyes looked at her in mute appeal that clawed at her battered heart.

It would be kinder to tell him the truth. Then at least the parting would be mutual.

But she couldn't do it.

This way, at least she would leave with her dignity intact. Illusions were important. She spent her days creating illusions out of paper and fabric, making environments out of empty boxes of drywall and plywood. Illusions could sustain you when everything else was falling apart.

"I love you, Tara."

He looked directly into her eyes, imploring, begging her to hear him and believe, to echo his words and join him in his fantasy world of their future together.

But she'd heard those words before.

I love you.

Maybe he thought he meant it, but he'd be singing another tune once he found out that she was barren.

What a lovely word, so biblical. Barren women had been despised and abandoned since the beginning of time. And even if she wasn't, history had proven that she wasn't really lovable. At least not in the way that someone would want to stay with her for their whole life.

Gordon had said, "I love you" to her a couple of times. Looking back, she didn't really believe it. He'd only said it on those rare occasions when she'd tried to pressure him into some kind of commitment. After all, how long did he expect her to wait for him to propose to her? But an "I love you" had worked nicely to shut her up.

She wondered how often people truly meant those three words when they said them.

Three little words were not much to hang a life on. No. Even if Jesse really did love her now—right now, at this moment—his love would wither and fade and he'd be left with nothing but distaste and anger that he'd been led astray by a carefully decorated facade that looked like a woman but wasn't really.

She shrugged her shoulders carefully. They were stiff, barely willing to obey her instructions.

"I'm sorry, Jesse. I feel I've misled you. I didn't mean to give you any false impressions now or in the past."

"My fault I suppose." Jesse was looking down at the table. "I guess when you want something badly enough you just kid yourself into believing it." They both looked at the blueprints of his big house. A house perfect for a happy family to grow and blossom in. Tears blurred Tara's eyes.

She had to leave. Right now.

She rose quickly, her chair scraping loudly against

the floor.

"I have to go. I'm sorry, Jesse, I truly am." Her voice cracked and she quickly cleared her throat and turned away from him, looking for where she had left her handbag.

"I'm sorry, too, Tara. More than you'll ever know. I wish my love would be enough for both of us. But I can't make you do something you don't want to do. You know your own mind." His voice rang hollow with sadness. Tara took a deep breath. Another minute and she'd be out of here, in her car, free, able to cry the river that was threatening to overflow its banks.

Jesse looked out the window. "You can't drive in this weather, Tara, it's too dangerous." The rain poured down in sheets. Even the dogs were all inside.

"I can't stay."

"I know you can't." He looked at her so sadly she thought for a moment that she was going to break. But she held firm. "The guesthouses are full tonight, but there's an apartment above the barn that's all made up."

"That would be fine. I'll leave as soon as the rain eases up."

Jesse didn't say anything. He picked up a big umbrella and led the way to the front door. As he turned to her his eyes were black with sorrow. She had put that sorrow there, again. She really didn't deserve to live. But she would, and so would he.

Jesse ushered her under the umbrella with him and she half expected to feel his arm around her shoulders as he led her to the barn, but it stayed firmly by his side. She knew he believed her, that her performance had been thoroughly convincing. After all, there was nothing between them but a few brief encounters, not a single one of them initiated by her.

She'd tried to avoid him, she really had. She'd known the whole thing was all wrong, right from the beginning.

Jesse led her into the apartment and briefly showed her where everything was. She had his phone number if she needed anything.

"I'm sorry, Jesse," said Tara, as he prepared to leave. Every inch of her body and soul ached.

"I know you are. I'm sorry, too." He paused, swallowing. "I wish you luck in life, Tara. I don't know what you want, but I hope you find it." There was no trace of mockery in his voice.

"Thanks. I hope you find what you want, too, Jesse."

The terrible look on his face made it painfully obvious to both of them that what he wanted was standing right there before him, in a rain-spattered suit, saying goodbye to him. Goodbye forever. Have a nice life.

Tara felt a sob rising in her throat and she turned quickly away from him.

Go, Jesse! Please! Go now!

He hesitated for a moment. Then as if he had heard her thoughts he turned slowly and left the room, closing the door softly behind him.

So that was it. The end.

Jesse let the rain run over his face, drenching his clothes, soaking him in its chilly embrace.

Once again he'd deluded himself into thinking that there was a future for him and Tara Kent. The power of his dream was so strong it hadn't really occurred to him that she wouldn't share it.

He could see that she liked him. There was no mistaking the way her eyes lit up with joy when they were together. She'd tried to fight her attraction to him, but it was real all right. But that wasn't necessarily enough, and for Tara it obviously wasn't enough.

An animal trainer. Well, he was an animal trainer and a damn good one too. It was a shame, a damn shame, but if she couldn't see that what they had was something rare and special, there was damn all he could do about it.

Oh, God. She pressed her hands to her mouth. She'd done it.

She had to have a cigarette, and she had to have one now. She'd lasted two months without one, but there was no way she was going to make it through tonight without the comforting crutch of smoke in her lungs and nicotine in her bloodstream.

The tears she'd been expecting hadn't even come. She was in some sort of shock. She knew she still had a stale pack in the glove compartment of her Porsche. She'd seen them when she'd shoved her most recent insurance card in there, and she hadn't got around to removing them yet.

She noticed that Jesse had left the umbrella dripping in a corner. He'd get soaked on the way back.

Don't think about him!

She picked up the umbrella, let herself out of the door and went down the stairs and out to her car.

As she stood in the barn aisle her hands shook so much it took her five tries to get her lighter to work.

The tobacco flared as she lit it, and she inhaled deeply.

Ugh! She coughed. It was disgusting. She flapped at the smoke with one hand, driving it away from her eyes. She was out of practice. Maybe the next puff would be better. She inhaled tentatively and the smoke seared her lungs.

Where was the comforting buzz she craved? She heard a horse shifting in one of the stalls. She tried again, inhaling deeply. No. It wasn't working. She stubbed the cigarette out underfoot and contemplated driving back home in the rain. So what if she got into a car wreck? Her life was a worthless waste of time anyway.

But she was too sensible to do that.

She'd always been sensible. Maybe that was part of her problem. Maybe if she'd been a bit more reckless she wouldn't be standing here, alone, with a nasty taste in her mouth and the prospect of a lifetime of spinsterhood ahead of her.

She climbed back up the stairs to the apartment and stretched out on top of the sheets of the neatly made bed.

She was exhausted.

She had to stay awake so she'd be able to drive away when the storm stopped.

But maybe it wouldn't hurt if she closed her weary, red eyes for a few seconds.

The smoke alarm woke her. The piercing shrill seared through her skull, making her leap to her feet.

Fire!

The overhead light had gone out, leaving her in thick darkness. Rain still hammered down outside.

The power must have gone out. She tried to shake off the fog of pain and misery that hung about her and focus her energies on getting out of the pitch-black room.

Where the hell was the door?

She could smell smoke, but she couldn't tell where it was coming from and there was no moonlight for her to make any sense of the strange room. She hadn't been paying attention when she'd seen it in the light. She'd had her mind on other matters.

She remembered that terrible look of sadness on Jesse's face. He looked like she'd stuck a knife in his gut. She'd stuck a knife in his heart, and her own.

Focus!

She moved away from the bed, groping with her hands. She tripped over the umbrella she'd left lying on the floor and stumbled and fell, sprawling out over the hard wood. Pain stung the palms of her hands as she scrambled to her feet again.

"Where's the door?" she cried. The smoke grew thicker. The fire must be somewhere in the barn below her.

Her cigarette.

Oh, God, she really did deserve to die. And now maybe she would.

But not without putting up a fight.

Sliding her feet along the floor to avoid tripping again, she inched forward in the darkness. Although her eyes were growing accustomed to the gloom, the smoke was now so thick that visibility was only a couple of feet. If she didn't get out right now, she was going to succumb to smoke inhalation.

She dropped to her hands and knees where the smoke was thinner. She knew the door was right over there, on the far side.... Ouch! She banged her head on the leg of a table and the pain stung her temple.

She could feel tears welling in her eyes, which were burning with the acrid smoke. Forcing herself to keep moving, she crawled forward past the table.

The door! She felt the frame first, then the smooth metal. The door led to the outside. If she could open it, then she could get down the stairs and be free. She groped for the handle and turned it.

It didn't open.

She rattled the handle. She fiddled with the catch underneath the knob. She felt up and down the door looking for another lock. She rattled the handle again. Then she began to sob.

Suddenly she was knocked backward, crashing down hard against the wood floor as the door flew open. Jesse's arms picked her up and carried her out into the pounding rain, which felt like the healing water of baptism into a new life.

Her sobs were interrupted by terrible racking coughs as her lungs struggled to purge themselves of the thick, white smoke.

"The horses should all be outside, but I've got to count them to make sure none of them ran into the barn. You stay here. Don't move!" Jesse left her sitting in the rain, on the wet grass. She shuddered, hardly able to believe that she was alive after such a narrow escape.

She turned to look at the barn behind her. Flames were already licking out of two of the lower windows. They were probably consuming all of Jesse's cherished mementos, his shelves of trophies and his pictures of his beloved horses.

Tara hung her head and wiped a wet hand over her

face.

Smoking in a barn, surrounded by flammable hay and straw. Anyone who did that really was too stupid to live.

Then she remembered the horse. She'd heard it while she was smoking. She remembered the sound of it shifting in one of the stalls. Someone must have put it in there without telling Jesse.

She scrambled to her feet on the slippery grass and hurried through the driving rain toward the burning building. She wondered if Jesse had called the fire department. Even if he had, there wasn't much hope that they would arrive in time to save anything. But if she could, she'd save that horse.

Racking her brain for which direction the horse sound had come from, she scaled a wooden fence and ran around the outside of the barn. Yes! There it was. The stall was filling with smoke but the top half of the dutch door to the outside was open.

She fiddled with the metal latch and opened the bottom half of the door.

"Come on, boy, come outside!" She couldn't understand why the horse didn't leave the smoky stall. She could see the flames on the far side of the interior stall door. Any moment the shavings in his stall would catch fire.

"Come on!" The horse was massive, intimidating, and his backside was to her. Steeling her courage she slid into the stall and reached up for its mane.

"Please come!" The horse tossed its head and she lost her grip. "You'll burn in here!" She reached for the mane again and tried to tug the horse backward, but it remained firmly in place.

In desperation she moved herself in front of the

horse and pushed hard against its chest.

"Go!" she shouted. The horse backed up a step. The noise of the roaring flames inside the barn was deafening. "Go!" The horse backed up another step, and she pushed harder.

Yes! The horse was outside, and she ran out and slammed and bolted the door behind her to prevent it going back in. As the lock slid back into place she saw the shadow of a man dash across the courtyard toward the guest cottages. "Hey, who's there?" It wasn't Jesse, and she was pretty sure no one else was at the ranch when she arrived. There had been no cars in the parking area except hers and Jesse's truck.

"Jesse, be careful, there's someone here!" Her words got lost in the pounding rain as a sharp blast of pain shot through her skull. She slumped to the wet ground, the rain drops pelting down on her as she drifted out of her senses.

She awoke in a hospital emergency room but was so tired that she kept falling asleep while they were examining her. Once they'd moved her to a private room she slept like the dead, probably drugged to the eyeballs. Her head throbbed where she'd been hit, by a piece of metal similar to a pry bar, they'd said. She was lucky not to have a fracture, and they were still worried about concussion.

As she awoke she heard raised voices outside her room. She still felt groggy, either from the blow to her head or the medication they'd given her. It was Jesse's voice. Her pulse quickened, and she strained to make out the words.

"But this is her mother. I know it's not visiting hours yet and Tara needs rest, but couldn't her mom just go in to see her?"

"Be quiet, sir, you'll wake the patient."

"I'm sorry, but it just seems… All right we'll go back to the waiting room."

"Wait!" Tara called out. "Mom!"

The door opened and her mom walked into the room.

"Oh, honey. Thank goodness you're awake. They're so worried about concussion."

"I think I'm okay. Just a little woozy."

Her eyes wandered back to the open door where Jesse stood, his face creased with worry.

"The doctor's coming," called a nurse's voice. "He'll give you an update now that the patient is awake."

"I had a cigarette." She had to get the confession out. "I could have started the fire."

"You didn't. Someone had poured gasoline all around the barn, around my house, and they were on their way to the cottages when you were hit. There were two of them. I tackled the one who hit you and the other ran off, but the police caught him. They're both in custody right now."

"What a relief. But why?"

"Mrs. Wicklow," the doctor entered, a spry older man, and shook her mother's hand. "Mr, er," he looked at Jesse.

"West, a friend." They shook hands.

"Well, the news is good, what we have of it. There's still a risk of concussion so Tara will have to remain here for another day under observation. But the head wound appears to be superficial and should heal quickly. Her pregnancy appears to be unaffected by the fall."

"My what?"

"Your pregnancy." The doctor looked at Tara, and she saw an expression of amusement grow in his face as he realized she had no idea what he was talking about.

"I'm not pregnant." Her voice sounded like it was coming from very far away.

Oh, yes, you are. About three weeks. In fact there's a distinct possibility that there are two of them in there."

"But I'm menopausal."

"You are not. You are also irrefutably and indisputably pregnant."

12

"I can't believe you really thought I wouldn't want you if you couldn't have children." Jesse shook his head.

She was in Jesse's bed, back at his house. "But you said that was why you broke up with your ex-girlfriend. I didn't want you to grow to resent me for not being able to give you the children you wanted."

"That was totally different. She didn't *want* them. That's what I couldn't relate to. Wanting them and not being able to have them is another story altogether. There's nothing you can do about that. That's just life." He kissed her softly on the lips again. "I'm still mad at you for almost ruining our future together. And you should never have gone back into that burning barn."

He shook his head and let out a wistful sigh. "When you yelled out, I turned and saw that man hit you. The police have determined that he's the rancher who was renting my brother's land. He tried to frame Bowie for murder—with help from my dad's foreman, who needed to get rid of a troublesome girlfriend—so he could keep using his land. Then when he couldn't get rid of him he set his sights on my land."

"Why didn't he just go rent somewhere else?"

"Turns out he and the foreman have had a sweet little money-making operation running for years now. The foreman rented him Bowie's land at way below market rates and the rancher gave him big kickbacks in cash. They'd kiss that gravy train goodbye if he couldn't stay on West land. Until this year Bowie was too busy with the rodeo circuit to notice, and my dad doesn't care about anything except his oil profits and stock investments, so he got away with it."

"Will they go to prison?"

"They're still trying to pin the murder on one or both of them, but arson is a serious charge, and so is attempted murder, so they'll go down for something."

"What a relief. I'm glad they were able to save the house." The stone cladding had kept the fire from taking hold and most of the damage could be fixed by pressure washing.

He nodded. "And you saved my horse, I'll never forget that."

The horse she had saved was Dante, his oldest equine friend. After he was done yelling at her for being fool enough to go back into a burning building, he'd thanked her with tears in his eyes.

"Dante has a lot to answer for," said Tara. "He didn't want to leave even though the flames were almost in his stall."

"Horses are like that. The barn is familiar to them, so their instinct is to stay there or even run back into it regardless of the danger."

"Hmm, reminds me of someone I know. Someone who let himself get burned three times by a certain stuck-up blonde."

"Yeah, really. I should get my head examined.

Falling in love with a woman who's too proud to tell me she doesn't think she can have children."

Tara shrugged and made a wry expression. "I know I need to work on my obsession with appearing flawless."

"Perfection is boring anyway. I bet you'll have a cute little scar on your forehead that will make you prettier than ever."

Tara grimaced and touched her bandage. "I'll have to choose a heavy wedding veil."

"You can pick whatever kind of veil you want. I want you to have the wedding of your dreams."

"Oh, dear. You haven't seen my dreams. I've put a lot of thought into my wedding over the years."

"Good. I want to be wrapped up in every one of those dreams. I want to make all your dreams come true." He leaned forward and kissed her again, slowly and softly, both of them savoring their newfound intimacy. "And it looks like two of them are well on their way." They both looked down at her belly.

Jesse looked up at her, a curious expression on his face.

"How come you didn't realize you were pregnant? You must have missed your period."

"I was taking the Pill. I usually skipped the placebo days so I didn't have to deal with bleeding, so I wasn't expecting a period. It explains why I've been so tired, too. Usually I love to exercise but lately all I want to do is lounge around."

"Lounge away. I'm here to wait upon your every whim."

"Well, if you put it that way…"

"Another bowl of butter-pecan ice cream with maple syrup?"

"I was thinking of something even sweeter." She licked her lips slowly, looking directly into Jesse's eyes. He blinked, his mouth settling into his familiar crooked smile, and he leaned his face closer to hers.

As his lips covered her own she reached for the fly of his jeans and unzipped them, pushing them down over his hips.

"Are you sure you're up for this?" he rasped, his eyes dark with desire.

"I'm more than sure."

Their lovemaking was gentle and tender, a slow build to a warm fire that consumed them both and made the love between them shine just a little brighter.

Afterward they spread Jesse's house plans out on the tangled sheets and shared their thoughts on the bedrooms and playroom that would accommodate their growing family.

"I can't wait." Jesse held her hand. The warm brown depths of his eyes shone with happiness. Happiness that she had put there and that she intended to keep there for the rest of their lives together.

"Neither can I."

EPILOGUE

"Oh, goodness, doesn't she look beautiful?" Tara felt emotion surge inside her as Lucy emerged from the barn. Her shiny dark curls framed a face glowing with happiness. Diamond-tipped cowgirl boots peeked from beneath Lucy's white satin dress as she and Bowie walked along a path of rice-paper petals to the frothy white gazebo set up for the ceremony. The trees around the property sparkled with white lights, and red and white bows ornamented the wood fencing. "I think I'm going to cry."

"At least now you know it's pregnancy wreaking havoc with your emotions, not menopause." Melody shot her a sideways glance. "I'm not drinking one sip of the water around here. Two pregnant shotgun brides in one winter? The West men need a good spanking if you ask me." Mischief twinkled in her eyes.

Tara felt a smile conquer her tears. "The West men are hard to resist." Bowie looked rakishly gorgeous, wearing his tuxedo jacket with jeans and boots, much like Jesse had to Melody's wedding.

Bowie and Lucy held hands while they repeated

the vows they'd written, under the watchful eye of the pastor.

Tara would be doing the same thing soon, at her own wedding to Jesse. Her heart squeezed when Bowie and Lucy were pronounced husband and wife, and the crowd roared when they kissed.

"Your gazebo will be more tasteful, won't it, darling?" Melody squinted at the explosion of white tulle ornamented with white doves and white roses. "I know you're madly in love, but there's no need to throw away all sense of propriety."

"I think it's pretty, but I'm planning to use all living decorations for mine. The florist suggested grapevine. They can bring a live grapevine arbor where the roots are in elegant containers, apparently."

"With grapes on?"

"I'm not sure they'll have grapes that early in the year, but the leaves are real."

Melody looked unconvinced. "You're not going to wear cowgirl boots, are you?"

Tara smiled. "I just found some Jimmy Choo ones."

"You are crazy in love."

"I am. And I'm really growing as a person. You have no idea how much more relaxed I am living out here. Jesse and I walk around together and check all the animals first thing in the morning and last thing at night. It's so peaceful. And I don't have to go hide in a coffee shop every time a prospective buyer comes to the old house."

"That mausoleum to your relationship with Gordon."

"It does feel like some sort of grim shrine compared to our life here." She sighed. "I never would have believed I could be this happy."

"You'll have your hands full with twins and the TV show."

"They're shooting the entire season in six weeks, starting in Februrary, so it will be all wrapped by the time I'm even getting big."

"You'll be in L.A. for six weeks?"

"Nope. I told them I couldn't come to L.A., so they're shooting around Austin and the hill country. We're very 'in' here, apparently. They're lining up the houses now. I've been sending them design plans and choosing colors and materials. All I have to do is show up and shoot. And we're using my line of paint for everything. Ace Hardware has just ordered the full line and placed an order with the factory, so instead of me owing them money, it's rolling in."

"See? I told you everything would work out. And here comes that sexy husband I found for you."

Tara turned and smiled to see Jesse, looking radiant and gorgeous—as usual—in his tux and jeans. "You found for me?"

"Credit where credit's due, sweetie. I practically shoved you into his arms, didn't I, Jesse?"

Tara felt Jesse's arms slide around her waist from behind. Warmth and relaxation flowed through her, along with the familiar sparkle of desire.

Jesse's low voice filled her ears. "Neither of us needed any shoving. Some things are just meant to be, even if they take a while." He kissed her cheek softly. "All's well that ends well."

"Even if it takes two reunions and twelve years." Melody shook her head and sighed.

Jesse twirled Tara around until his arms circled her waist, holding her close. Her heart swelled with joy.

He kissed her lips gently and a quick flash of tongue made her heart skip a beat. "Especially then."

THE END

To learn more about Jennifer Lewis' books, including the upcoming Royal Secrets series, join the new release mailing list at www.jenlewis.com.

ABOUT THE AUTHOR

Jennifer Lewis loves heat in all its forms including spicy food, steamy temperatures and smoking hot heroes. She is a USA TODAY bestselling author and her books have been translated into more than twenty languages. She lives in sunny South Florida and when she's not sitting at her laptop she can often be found at the beach. Read more about her books and join her new release mailing list at www.jenlewis.com.